Barry Crump wrote his fi[...] Man, in 1960. It became [...] numerous other books w[...] famous and best-loved New[...] Cash, who features in *Hang on a Minute Mate,* Crump's second book. Between them, these two books have sold over 400,000 copies and continue to sell at an amazing rate some 30 years later.

Crump began his working life as a professional hunter, culling deer and pigs in some of the ruggedest country in New Zealand. After the runaway success of his first book, he pursued many diverse activities, including goldmining, radio talkback, white-baiting, television presenting, crocodile shooting and acting.

As to classifying his occupation, Crump always insisted that he was a Kiwi bushman.

He published 25 books and was awarded the MBE for services to literature in 1994.

Books by Barry Crump

A Good Keen Man (1960)
Hang on a Minute Mate (1961)
One of Us (1962)
There and Back (1963)
Gulf (1964) – now titled *Crocodile Country*
Scrapwaggon (1965)
The Odd Spot of Bother (1967)
No Reference Intended (1968)
Warm Beer and Other Stories (1969)
A Good Keen Girl (1970)
Bastards I Have Met (1970)
Fred (1972)
Shorty (1980)
Puha Road (1982)
The Adventures of Sam Cash (1985)
Wild Pork and Watercress (1986)
Barry Crump's Bedtime Yarns (1988)
Bullock Creek (1989)
The Life and Times of a Good Keen Man (1992)
Gold and Greenstone (1993)
Arty and the Fox (1994)
Forty Yarns and a Song (1995)
Mrs Windyflax and the Pungapeople (1995)
Crumpy's Campfire Companion (1996)
As the Saying Goes (1996)
A Tribute to Crumpy: Barry Crump 1935–1996 is an
anthology of tributes, extracts from Crump's books,
letters and pictures from his private photo collection.

All titles currently (1997) in print.

BARRY CRUMP

THE ADVENTURES OF SAM CASH

BARRY CRUMP

THE ADVENTURES OF SAM CASH

Illustrated by Dennis Turner

Hodder Moa Beckett

First published in 1985 by Beckett Publishing

This edition published in 1997

ISBN 1-86958-548-8

© 1985 Barry Crump

Published by Hodder Moa Beckett Publishers Limited
[a member of the Hodder Headline Group]
4 Whetu Place, Mairangi Bay, Auckland, New Zealand

Typeset by TTS Jazz, Auckland

Cover photo: NZPL/Evan Collis

Printed by Griffin Paperbacks, Australia

Contents

from

Hang on a Minute Mate

There and Back

SAM

Sam Cash looked at his old woman the way a man looks at a steep ridge he's got to climb on a hot day. It was a long time to spend in one place. Time wasted with a woman who had come to represent only a tremendous amount of noise.

Too much money in her family for a man to have got a fair go in the first place, he reflected. If a man had any go in him he'd take her at her word and head off down country again. Back to the old life with plenty of hard work and no nagging woman on a man's back all the time. He sat by the fire, thinking about places he'd been and things he'd done.

"I'm going to bed," she barked through the remembered noise of a woolshed Sam was working in just then. "I suppose you're going to sit there smoking those filthy cigarettes all night. Why can't you be like other men and keep decent hours? Up half the night and waking up bad-tempered in the morning. You can sleep in the spare room if you're going to carry on like this. It's disgraceful! Always telling lies and skiting about the silly things you've done. Frittering away your life, that's what you're doing . . .!"

In his mind Sam rode a muddy horse through a gate in a long row of pines and dismounted by a small hut on a river-flat.

"You could clout a man if he talked to you like that," he muttered to the horse, as the bedroom door slammed behind his loved one. Queer, though, how a man can get so used to a thing that he misses it when it's gone, whether he likes it or not. He'd probably even miss the Old Girl if he shot through on her, but it was hard to imagine. He dug the fire in the ribs with a piece of wood and rolled himself another smoke.

How long is it since a man stood on a jigger-board or boiled his billy over a manuka fire, or swore at his dogs or drank beer in a pub that didn't close at six on the knocker and shove you out on the footpath with nothing to do but go home and listen to the bitching? Close on eight months!

11

And what was it she said this morning? Something about how if it wasn't for her old man they'd be out on the street. And then Sam had to "go and repay all he's done for us by threatening to do that with his truck and telling him to do it with his job. Filthy language and wicked ungratefulness. Why don't you go back and live like the pig you tried to turn me into? I don't know why I ever married you. Never shaving and going round like a filthy hobo. No wonder you can't get jobs! And me having to ask Daddy for money all the time."

Daddy! — What's happened to a man? wondered Sam.

He sat looking into the fire for a long time. He slept there.

JACK

An unregistered Model A truck with a boiling radiator chuttered round the corner and stopped with a cloud of white steam geysering into the early morning darkness from somewhere under the bonnet. Jack struck a match in front of a glassless alarm-clock that hung on a piece of wire from the dashboard. Then he climbed out and got a stick off the back to dip the petrol-tank with.

Three o'clock in the morning and out of gas. If he didn't get his bomb out of this town, whatever it was, and into the country by daylight he'd get run in and they'd probably get in touch with his old man, and there'd be a hell of a stink. Especially when they found out about him getting the sack from the garage.

In another four years, eight months, three weeks and two days he would have been a certified mechanic, if he'd checked the chocks under the new Austin that tipped off the lubrication hoist yesterday. It seemed like a year since he'd signed for his pay and driven south without knowing where he was going. Or caring much either. Now he didn't even know where he was. And there was no going back after that letter he'd posted home as he passed through Warkworth.

He walked along to a car that was parked on the roadside, lifting a couple of quart milk bottles off a gatepost on the way. The cap on the tank wasn't locked and he was looking in the boot for a siphon-hose when a prowl car slid round the bend and pinned him with a spotlight to the scene of his first crime. He kicked the milk bottles on to the grass verge with the side of his foot as the black car stopped beside him. The light shifted from his face to the hand in which he still clutched the petrol cap, and he saw that there were two black uniforms in the car.

"Well now," said the one with the light, getting out and flashing a notebook. "What've we got here? That your car lad?"

"Not exactly. I was just having a look at it."

"A look, eh? A look into the petrol-tank. What's your name?"

"Jack Lilburn."

"Got your driver's licence with you?"

"No."

"Where do you live?"

"Whangarei — I'm looking for a job."

"Unemployed eh? And whose car is this?"

"I suppose it belongs to the people in this house."

"Well, let's just go and make sure, shall we? Come on Blake."

The other uniform got out of the car and Jack walked between them to see the car owner. At their second knock somebody moved inside the house and a light went on over their heads. The door opened and a tall, thin, whiskery man of about forty said, "What the hell?"

Then he saw the uniforms and Jack's frightened face. He looked at Jack.

"That your green Chevrolet, registered number eight five eight three seven three, parked outside here?" asked the first policeman.

"Yeah, why?" said the thin man slowly, still looking at Jack.

"We caught this character in the act of interfering with it. He had the boot open and the cap of the petrol-tank in his hand. Now if you would just come along to the station with us . . ."

"Hell, what a time of the day to run out of gas!" said the thin man to Jack, ignoring the policeman. "Hang on a tick and I'll give you a hand. There's usually a tin lying around in the washhouse here somewhere."

"I'm afraid I'll have to ask you to come down to headquarters with us, sir," said the policeman, looking a bit annoyed. "We're placing this chap under arrest, and we'll need your statement."

"What!" said the thin man. "Don't you think he's had enough trouble for one night? First the poor sod runs out of juice, and then you blokes have to pounce on him. As a matter of fact I told young Bill here a couple of weeks ago that any time he wanted a gallon . . ."

"I wouldn't advise that now, sir," interrupted the policeman, holding up his hand. "We won't keep you long. There's been too much of this sort of thing going on around here lately. You'll get no thanks for trying to help these types. They've got no respect for anyone's . . ."

"Now just you hang on there a minute, mate!" said the thin man, coming out on to the porch and standing close up to the policeman, who stepped back and stood on the second step, looking up at him. You can't come round here waking a man up in the early hours of the morning and then practically calling him a liar to his face. By strike, there'll be trouble over this, believe me! You blokes have overstepped the mark this time, and I'm just the wrong bloke to do it to. One more insult and I'll come down to the station all right. And I'll have Harvey Wilson himself with me, and you know what that means!"

"We're only doing our job, sir." The policeman spoke much less aggressively and avoided the thin man's eyes. "It's our duty to investigate any suspicious circumstances."

"Well, you've investigated them, haven't you? Young Bill here's been a friend of the family for I don't know how long. Trouble with you blokes is you won't admit when you've made a blue."

"Since you refuse to co-operate with us we'll consider the matter closed for the time being — but if we catch this character round the streets at this hour again I'll remember this."

"So!" said the thin man. "It's threats now, is it? I'm not sure that I won't see Harvey Wilson first thing in the morning, after all. I'm not standing for any more of this sort of nonsense!"

The policemen left, and on turning from watching them climb the steps to the gate, Jack saw that the thin man was grinning delightedly.

"Er — thanks very much . . ." he began embarrassedly.

"Ar, forget it," said the thin man, still grinning. "I wouldn't see a man in the cart for a lousy couple of gallons of petrol." He sat on the top step and began rolling a cigarette. Jack noticed for the first time that he was fully dressed.

"Y'know, it reminds me of the time a mate and I ran out of gas fair slap in the middle of Hamilton. Ten o'clock at night, and we never had a cracker. Heading for a job at Kawerau, we were. My mate said he'd take the tin and see if he could half-inch a gallon or two, and I went with him to keep an eye on things. Well, the first chariot my mate claps his eye on is a taxi standing outside a coffee shop, and he bowls up, lifts the cap and shoves the pipe into this bloke's tank, saying we had more chance of getting away with it if we swiped the stuff publicly. Just when we looked like pulling it off a bloke comes out of this coffee joint and says: 'Hey, who told you you could take that petrol out of there?'

" 'Who the hell do you think?' says my mate. 'The owner of the bloomin' car, of course!'

" 'Okay,' says the bloke. 'Don't get your back up, mate. I only drive for him. Never know what to expect from old Barney.'

" 'Anyone would think we were swipin' the blasted stuff, the way you come up and beller at a man!' says my mate. 'Here, hang on to this tin and I'll get ready to pull the hose out. Don't want to waste any. One of Barney's mates has run out of gas four mile out!'

"And this bloke gives us a hand to milk his boss's car. My mate reckoned he'd never laughed so much since his brother's pig-dogs got loose and followed him into the Waitawheta dance hall . . .!

"Now, let's see about this petrol of yours."

He found a hose and a two-gallon tin and they went up to the car. Waiting for the tin to fill, the thin man said, "Where you heading, son?"

"South."

"Yeah? Any particular place?"

"No. Just south."

"On your own?" The thin man seemed interested.

"Yeah, I'll have a look round for a job when I get down Taihape way."

"You'll do all right down there," said the thin man. "There's mustering, and shearing gangs this time of year. Fencing and scrub-cutting, packing, logging — any amount of jobs going. Never tell them you can't do a thing. Get stuck in and have a go. By the time they find out you've never done it before, you're doing it."

While they were pouring the third tin of petrol into Jack's little truck, the thin man, who'd been silent for a few minutes, suddenly said, "You got enough room for a passenger for down the line, mate?"

"Too right!" said Jack. "Far as you like."

"Right, I'll just nick down and grab a few hunks of gear and be right with you."

He returned in a few minutes with a shotgun and a full pack, threw them on the back of Jack's truck and stuck his hand across the bonnet.

"By the way, my name's Sam Cash."

"Mine's Jack Lilburn. Pleased to meet you."

"Same here."

As they swung out to drive off, Jack said, "Hey, what about your car?"

"I haven't got one," said Sam grinning. "I think that's the bloke next door's. Proper ratbag of a joker he is, too."

They laughed for half a mile.

"By the way, Sam, who's Harvey Wilson?"

"I think he was someone in a book I read once," replied Sam. They laughed for another half-mile.

"Good thing those johns didn't get a decent look at this bomb of yours," said Sam, folding a wad of paper to jam the window up. "We'd have had a job talking our way out of this little lot."

A Tidy Heap

They stopped in a small town for Sam to send a telegram to his "Old Hairpin", and returned to the truck to find a traffic cop standing by it, slapping the side of his leg with a ticket-book.

"Don't like the look of this," muttered Sam. "Just ignore him and if he says anything let me handle him."

Sam nodded to the officer and started climbing into the driver's seat.

"Hold it a minute there, will you," said the cop. "Has this vehicle got a warrant of fitness?"

"A warrant of fitness?" said Sam, looking surprised. "How the hell do you think a man could get a warrant for a thing like this? — no brakes, steering crook, doors flying open in all directions, tyres down to the canvas — and you ask us if we've got a warrant! No, we haven't got a warrant."

"Are you aware of the law regarding warrants of fitness for motor vehicles?"

"Officer," said Sam, "we've had more tickets for this old girl than she could carry. And every fine puts us just that much further from getting 'er done up. The money we've paid to you blokes would have bought me a new truck. Here we are, struggling along out there in the backblocks, eighty hours a week, and all our money going to pay fines for the only enjoyment we can get out of life. A little trip into town once a month or so. We've gone hungry out there officer — living on the dog tucker — to pay the penalty for our little bit of harmless fun." Sam waved an earnest arm towards a formidable expanse of mountainous bush country that wasn't there.

"You obviously haven't made much effort to get the thing fixed up. It's a menace to other road users. Look at it!"

"A menace?" cried Sam. "A menace! Do you know that when we bought the old girl, officer, she had two rope tyres; she had one spoke of the steering wheel left; she had no windscreen, there wasn't a sound board in her; she had two cracked pistons, no floor-boards, no seats, one headlight, leather big-end bearings, and she was going on one cylinder because all the valves were burnt out. She had fencing wire brake-rods and a piece of rope to work the throttle with because there was no accelerator. And you say we haven't made much effort. Why, young Bill here could tell you a thing or two about old Gertie. I'd like a quid for every mile he's walked behind her with a post."

"With a post?"

"Yes, officer, with a dirty big post. When we first got her every forward gear in her was shot to pieces. The only way to get her down a hill without harpooning something was to stick her in reverse and go down backwards. When she got going too fast I'd yell out and young Bill here would drop his post behind the wheels and get out of the way. You've got no idea the work and expense we've put into this old bus to get her in the condition she's in today, officer. And one day we hope to have her one of the tidiest little heaps in the district."

For a moment Jack thought the tremor in Sam's voice was genuine. The traffic cop stopped slapping his leg with the ticket-book and looked at Sam with a frown that was trying hard not to be a grin.

"We came into town today, officer," continued Sam, "to order a complete new set of brake linings and a wheel bearing, but it looks as though we'll have to spend the money on another fine." He turned away and leaned on a sagging mudguard, the very picture of a man who has just been confronted with defeat and ruin.

"Look, I don't want to be too tough on you," said the traffic cop. "I suppose you've got a driver's licence?"

"Officer," said Sam, turning to face him again. "A man who can navigate a machine like old Gertie here for eleven years without a single prang is qualified to drive anything on wheels. As a matter of fact I've been too ashamed to ask for one in case they laughed at me. And the spare few bob I've scraped together from time to time have gone towards paying fines or some little thing to make Gertie a safer and more roadworthy machine." He turned and fondly adjusted an ill-fitting bonnet clip.

"Okay, okay," said the officer. "How about your registration sticker? What happened to that?"

"Do you know, officer," said Sam, "you won't believe this, but a week or two back we tried shoving a batten through a gap in the floor-boards to slow the old girl up on the hills. The batten caught on a rock in the road and the other end flew out of Bill's hand and went fair through the windscreen. We never did find the bit that had the sticker on it. We got this windscreen off a wrecker for thirty bob."

"I'll tell you what I'll do with you," said the traffic officer, frowning sternly at Sam. "How far away do you live?"

"Forty-six mile, officer."

"Right. I'll give you temporary permission to drive the thing forty-six miles. If I see you in town with it again without a registration sticker, a warrant of fitness and a driver's licence, I'll put both you and your Gertie off the road. Does your speedo work?"

"Yes," said Sam, proudly. "We've done 'er up."

The officer took the speedometer reading, added forty-six miles, and wrote out a note saying Sam could drive that distance.

"What's your name?"

"Harvey Wilson," replied Sam.

"They're getting tough these days," said Sam as they drove away. "One time it was twice as easy. We'll have to stop along here and unscrew the speedo cable. Here, stick this note where it won't get dirty, Jack. We're likely to need it for a fair while yet. What was the name of that town anyway? We'll have to steer clear of there in future. That cop likes his job a bit too much if you ask me. The kind of joker who shoots fantails for fun. Keep 'er moving, Jack. At this rate we'll soon be in Taupo."

"Where are you thinking of settling down, Sam?"

"Anywhere suits me, Jack. As long as it's not more than a few weeks I'll tackle anything there's a quid in."

"Sounds like a good idea, Sam, but do you think there'd be enough jobs for us to do?"

"More than enough," said Sam. "If we run out of a job we'll make one by wrecking something that'll have to be fixed."

25

"We couldn't get away with that too many times."

"Anything's better than being tied down to one place," said Sam decidedly. "That'd kill off a man quicker than a cut throat.

"I've tried the settling down caper, Jack me boy. It doesn't work out. A while back I decided to give up travelling around and give the married life a fair go. I'd been carting the missus round from place to place with me for nearly six months and she was getting a bit restless to go into the home life business. You know, kids and cooking and all that sort of stuff.

"I scraped up a thousand quid and went to see one of them land agent blokes. Didn't like the look of him much, but he reckoned he had a nearly brand-new house just out of town that I could have for a thousand down and two hundred quid a year for so many years I lost count. Ten acres of ground went with the place but there was a bit of work needed to get it ready for cows and things.

"Before I could tell him I'd think it over he had me in his flash car and heading out to have a look at it. We called in and picked up the wife and he spouted on and on about what a good bargain we were getting.

"The place looked all right when we got there except that the ten acres was covered in tall scrub and ran up behind the house so steep that you could just about spit on the roof from the top. The house itself was a fair enough go. Everything was as good as he said it was, but I knew he was pulling a shrewdie on me somewhere. The way I got it worked out I was getting the place about six hundred quid too cheap. Didn't like it at all. I went through the house like a mob of sheep through a gateway — even lit a fire to see if the chimney smoked — but there was just nothing wrong with it. Then the wife says it's just the kind of place she's always wanted and that was that. We moved in a week later. Time payment furniture and everything!

"It was a nice little place all right. Good dirt in case I got to like the idea of a garden. No leaks or rotten floor-boards, sheltered, warm, comfortable — the works. I got a job handy at home, took a lunch with me in the mornings and got told off for not bringing the paper bag home for next day — women are funny about paper bags and lists of things from the store, Jack me boy. It's a bad sign

26

when they start that caper on you.

"I started cleaning up a bit of the scrub on weekends. Strike, that hill was steep! It was a waste of time cleaning it really because it wasn't going to be much good for anything anyway; but it was a handy little something to do when I wanted to get away from the paper bags and lists of things from the store for a while.

"I suppose I must have been picking away at it for about a month when one afternoon I thought I saw a shed through the scrub up ahead of me. I climbed up for a look and there was the biggest hunk of rock I've ever seen in all me born days. A dirty great hundred-ton boulder perched on the side of the hill, straight above our new house. And it looked as if the next breeze was going to set her rolling.

"I tell you, Jack me boy, it gave a man the Joe Blakes just to look at it. I sat on the side of the hill, rolled myself a smoke and wondered how I was going to tell the missus. Decided she'd better have a look for herself so I cut all the scrub from round the rock and went down to the house. I bowled into the kitchen and told the wife to have a look out the window. She just about flipped her lid. Thought the rock was on its way down. It looked like it too. I couldn't see how it could stay up there. Most of it seemed to be hanging out over the house."

"I remember about that," said Jack. "Didn't they make a cartoon about it?"

"That's right," said Sam. "The paper paid me a tenner for the cartoon rights. Well, we crept around the place getting our most important gear out to the gate. The missus was in a proper state. Gave her the horrors to think we'd been sleeping at night under that stone. On my way out with a boxful of crockery I dropped it and the wife let out a mortal scream. She thought her time had come. Don't blame her, either. I was a bit on edge myself.

"We loaded the gear on to our old bus and drove into town. I pulled the door of that land agent's office open so hard the handle came off in my hand. The girl in the office said he was out of town for a few days but was there any message? On my way out I slammed the door so hard the glass panel with his name on cracked.

"The missus and I camped in a pub across the road from the land agent's office and waited till he came back, a couple of days later. As soon as he went into his office I rang him up.

" 'G'day there,' I says.

" 'Hullo. Hullo. Who's speaking?' he says.

" 'Sam Cash,' I tells him.

" 'Oh, yes,' he says. 'How's things, Mister Cash?'

" 'Fair enough,' I says.

" 'How's the house?' he says.

" 'Good,' I says.

" 'Ah. Splendid,' he says. 'Glad to hear everything's all right.'

" 'It's not,' I says.

" 'Why, what's the matter?' he says.

" 'Small matter of the pebble on the hill,' I says.

" 'Heavens!' he says. 'Has it come down? Anybody hurt?'

" 'Not yet,' I says.

" 'What do you mean?' he says.

" 'Can't make up my mind whether to put the bulls on to you or take it out of your hide,' I tells him.

" 'Now look here, Mister Cash,' he says. 'I'm sure we can settle this like gentlemen.'

" 'I don't feel like a gentleman,' I says, 'and you don't act like one, so that knocks that little idea on the head.'

" 'What's your complaint, Mister Cash?' he says. 'That stone's been there for years. It's as safe as a rock.'

" 'You'd better go and have a look at it,' I says, and hangs up.

"A few minutes later he roared off in his car to have a look. When he came back I got him on the blower again.

" 'Yes,' he says, 'I've just been out there. I didn't realise it was so overhanging. If you like I'll withdraw the place from sale and refund your money, less a month's rent, of course. Would you like to come down and talk it over in my office?'

"I could tell he had the wind up, so I said: 'No, I'd better not. It wouldn't be safe.'

" 'Why?' he says.

" 'I mightn't be responsible for what I did to you,' I says.

"Then he got really worried and wanted to know what I wanted him to do about it.

" 'I've got a list of expenses here,' I says.

" 'What expenses?' he says.

" 'Well,' I says, 'first there's a thousand quid I paid down on the place.'

" 'That's right,' he says.

" 'Then,' I says, 'there's four acres of scrub-cutting at five quid an acre.'

" 'I see that,' he says.

" 'Then there's the expense of finding another house,' I says. 'That'll be about fifty quid.'

" 'Yes,' he says.

" 'Then there's hotel bills,' I says.

" 'Yes,' he says.

" 'Then there's another fifty quid,' I says.

" 'What's that for?' he says.

" 'To keep my wife from going to the johns,' I says.

" 'No you don't,' he says. 'I won't pay it. That's blackmail!'

" 'She doesn't look at it that way,' I tells him. 'She reckons you exposed her life to danger just to make a few quid. She's away getting legal advice now.'

" 'All right,' he says. 'I'll consider it. Is that all?'

" 'Not quite,' I says. 'There's another fifty quid.'

" 'And what's that for?' he says.

" 'To keep *me* from going to the bulls,' I tells him. 'My life was exposed to danger too.'

" 'Now this has gone far enough,' he says. 'I don't mind reasonable expenses, but that's over the odds.'

" 'All right,' I says. 'I'll have to go now. I think our lawyer wants to go out with us to photograph that rock.'

" 'No, wait on,' he squeaks. 'I don't mind paying you a little something for your worry. How much do you think it is altogether?'

" 'I haven't finished yet,' I says.

" 'What else is there?' he yelps.

" 'There's loss of wages, and dry-cleaning for one pair of strides, and one slasher-handle, and one cup and saucer, and a hundred quid,' I says.

" 'What's the hundred quid for?' he croaks.

" 'Big house-warming party in the new house,' I says.

" 'Cut it out,' he says. 'That's nothing but barefaced blackmail!'

" 'Call it what you like,' I tells him. 'But the way I've got it worked out you're still making money on the deal.'

" 'How's that?' he says.

" 'Well,' I says, 'I reckon you'd get about two years up the hill for endangering our innocent lives. Supposing you make forty quid a week profit; in two years, that comes to about four thousand quid. By the time you pay me one thousand, three hundred and ninety-five pound six and fourpence you'll still have sixteen months' profit out of the next two years' work; and you won't be locked up.'

" 'You're a hard man, Mister Cash,' he says. But he must have had the wind up good and proper because he paid up that very day.

"And that was the only time I ever had the house buying business on. We went and lived in one of the wife's old man's houses after that and what I put up with for six months until you came along was enough to send a man fair round the screamin', meth-drinkin' bend. Should have got out of it years ago — ah, here's Taupo, Jack. Feel like a beer?"

"Too right," said Jack.

They pulled up outside a very old pub and walked into a deserted bar. Sam clicked a coin loudly on the bar and a tired barman came in the front door, climbed over the bar and reached for two glasses.

"Beer?" he asked.

Sam nodded and passed Jack the tobacco.

"What year were you born, lad?" asked the barman, eyeing Jack up and down.

"Now hang on a minute there, mate," interrupted Sam. "If you want to know a man's age why don't you ask him straight out? Bit tough when a twenty-four-year-old bloke can't come in for a quiet beer without having insults slung at him."

"No offence, mate," said the barman. "He does look a bit young at first glance."

"Well, I must admit you're not the first to be taken in by young

Jack's looks. Matter of fact he had me bluffed when I first met him," said Sam, subsiding. "You having one yourself?"

"Don't mind if I do," said the barman, reaching for a five ounce.

"Much doing in the way of work around here?" asked Sam, poking the empty glasses towards the barman with a dirty finger.

"Well, I heard Dan Hartshorne was starting a new logging contract this week if he could get the men. Can you knock a tree down? — Here, have this one with me."

"Can we knock a tree down, he asks us," scoffed Sam, turning to Jack with a surprised laugh. "If you'd seen us a week ago you'd know whether or not we could knock a tree down. Do you remember when Harvey Wilson got the big kauri logging contract up North Auckland way a couple of years back?"

"Did hear something about it now you mention it," said the barman. "Just forget the details now, but I think one of the contractors from here went up to have a look at it."

"That'll be the one," said Sam. "Clearing all the timber out of the valley to three chain above the proposed water line of the new dam they're going to put in there."

"That's right, now I remember," said the barman.

"Well, this time last week Jack and I were cross-cutting in the last stand of kauri they'll ever mill in this country. Some of the best sticks I ever saw in my life, and I've seen one or two, believe me. Twelve-foot cross-cut wouldn't look at some of those big fellers. Had to take the scarfs out in sections and blade them out of the way with a dozer — yeah, same again, thanks."

"Well, I reckon Dan'd be pretty glad to get hold of you blokes if you're looking for bush work. Of course, we haven't got any big stuff down this way like where you come from," he added, with a beery wink at Jack.

"We'd have to have a look at it first," said Sam doubtfully. "We wouldn't stay on a job five minutes if the dough's no good."

"Tell you what," said the barman. "Old Dan's on the blower up there. I'll give him a tinkle for you if you like."

"That's pretty decent of you, mate," said Sam. "But don't promise him anything. Just find out if he wants a couple of experienced bushmen. We might nick up and see him if he does."

The barman went out the back to ring up and Jack said, "But I've never chopped big trees down, Sam."

"You don't chop trees down, you saw them down; and you've been doing it all your life," said Sam.

"Dan says for you to go on up," said the barman, returning. "He'll be at the camp waiting for you."

"He's taking a fair bit for granted," grumbled Sam. "Still, I don't suppose it'll do any harm to go and have a look at the dump. How do we get there?"

"Three mile up here, turn in by a big white mail-box on your left and follow the pumice road till you see the camp in the valley. It's nine miles altogether."

"Well, thanks mate. We'll be seeing you," said Sam.

"Thanks for the beer," added Jack.

"She's right," said the barman. "Hope you get the job."

"Depends whether we want it or not," said Sam.

No Sense of Humour

Dan Hartshorne looked at Jack as though he was made of logs.

"Brought in a few things we found in your mailbox," said Sam, nodding to a couple of parcels on the truck.

"Thanks," boomed the log man. "You the boys from up north?"

"That's right," said Sam.

"Where's all your gear?" he asked, looking on the truck.

"You don't expect a man to use kauri gear on this stuff, do you?" said Sam incredulously, waving an arm towards the bush-covered hills that rolled endlessly back from the camp. "Our saws would be twice too big, and set and sharpened all different. We didn't even bring our axes!"

"Hmm, well, I s'pose I can fix you up with an axe each. Used a chainsaw before?"

"Had one of our own last year," said Sam. "Had to get rid of it. Too small for the kauri."

"Righto. I'll bring you down the stuff later. You can use the hut at the end there. You eat in the cookhouse and I'll take a couple of quid a week out of your pay."

"What are you paying us, Mister Hartshorne?" asked Sam.

"Same as usual. One and six a hundred for felling and breaking out."

"We were getting one and nine on the last job," said Sam doubtfully.

"I'll start you on one and six and if you do a good job I'll see about the extra threepence."

"He's a hard man," said Sam, as he and Jack threw their things on to the bunks and shelves in their little hut. "We'll have to handle him very carefully."

"Do we have to chop down a hundred trees for one and six?" asked Jack.

"No. We saw them down and get one and six for every hundred feet of timber in the logs."

"Can you really use a chainsaw, Sam?" asked Jack, worried at the prospect of an angry Mr Hartshorne.

"Ask me again this time tomorrow," said Sam, grinning as he put a match to the fire he'd got ready.

"And what's breaking out?"

"Oh, you just get the log ready and hook her on to the winch-rope when the tractor comes to snig her out to the skids."

"Skids?"

"That's the ramp where they load the logs on to the trucks. This sounds like him coming with the gear. Now don't forget — you scarf trees and cut them down with a saw. I'll show you the details tomorrow."

The boss gave them a small chainsaw, tins of oil and petrol, two new axes, and the rest of the day off to make their hut comfortable and sharpen the axes. He told them he'd be down in the morning to take them up to the workings and get them started on the job.

"He might make a fair enough boss, once we get him knocked into shape," remarked Sam, when Dan was barely out of earshot.

"Ever get into trouble by telling a boss you can do a job when you can't, Sam?" asked Jack as they lay in their bunks that night.

"Yeah, when I was a young feller — seventeen or eighteen I must have been — I answered an ad in the paper for a teamster.

"I must have been the only one who applied because I got the job. Huey Thomas was the bloke's name. Most miserable old coot I've ever worked for in all my born days, Jack. And I've worked for some mongrels in my time. Old Huey would have swiped the harness off a nightmare if he thought he could get away with it. The bloke who gave me a lift up there told me to count my fingers if Huey shook hands with me, but he didn't. The first thing he said when he saw me was that he never paid a man for the day he turned up on the job because half the day was gone before he got started and the other half was always wasted with him learning the ropes. And this was before he even knew what I'd come for. I might have been a stock agent for all he knew.

"I stuck my gear in an old fowl-house he'd furnished by adding a bunk and candle, and went with him down the paddock to where he had six dirty big Clydesdales hooked up in the blocks. He was

36

blasting stumps loose with gelignite and snigging them into heap
with the team.

" 'Ever handled a six-horse team, Sam?' he said.

"I didn't know Harvey Wilson in those days so I just told him
I'd been discing a few hundred acres of fern for a bloke in
Taranaki with a six-horse team.

" 'Never heard of anyone ever using six horses in the discs,' he
said. But he was too worried about the time to waste any asking
me any more about horses, which was just as well for me. The
nearest I'd ever come to handling a team was feeding out the hay
with Uncle Wally's two old nags in the konaki. Huey said to get
cracking on a dirty great sea of stumps and logs and snig them
into a heap he'd started in the gully. He reckoned I should have
cleaned up all the loose stumps by dark. It looked like a good
week's work to me but not knowing anything about the job I kept
me mouth shut. I grabbed the reins and said Git up! to the horses.

" 'What are y' doin'?' yelled Huey.

" 'What's wrong?' I says.

" 'Might be an idea to untie the lead horses from the fence,' he
says. 'They go better that way.'

"I untied them, got 'em turned round and headed up towards
the stumps.

" 'What are y' doin'?' yells Huey again.

" 'What's wrong?' I says again.

" 'Might be an idea to put a bit of weight on your strap,' he
says. 'It saves the horses getting their legs over the chains and
wrecking everything.'

"I grabbed the wire rope on the double-tree and set off again.

" 'What are y' doin'?' he yells.

" 'What's wrong?' I says.

" 'Might be an idea to hook that post on to the strap,' he says.
'It saves your hands getting ripped to bits on the burrs on the wire
rope. You after a bit of compo or something?'

"I dropped the reins and started walking across to get the post
he was pointing at.

" 'What are y' doin'?' he yells.

" 'Going to get the post,' I says.

" 'It might be an idea to hook your reins on to something,' he

37

says. 'Where do you think the horses are going to be when you get back?'

"I tied the reins to a lump of scrub and got the post hooked on.

" 'Might be an idea to tighten your checks a bit,' he says. 'They're a bit on the slack side.'

"I knew he was trying me out to see if I knew what checks were so I said:

" 'They look all right to me, mate!'

" 'Please yourself,' he says, 'but don't blame me if they get away on you.'

"In a little while I had it worked out that checks are the leads off the reins that go from the outside of one lead horse to the inside of the other lead horse's bit, so that both of them steer at the same time. I got the team up to an easy-looking stump, hooked them on and dragged it out. I headed them down to the heap with it, thinking the job wasn't going to be so hard after all.

" 'What are y' doin'?' yells Huey.

" 'What's wrong,' I says.

" 'Might be an idea to hook another half-dozen stumps on there,' he says. 'No wonder you needed six horses to pull a set of discs if that's all they'd drag.'

" 'Just getting the feel of the horses before I load them too much,' I says.

" 'Might be an idea to let them get the feel of a load while you're about it,' he says. 'There's enough time been wasted around here already.'

"I couldn't figure out how to get the team with the stump reversed back to the other six stumps I had to hook on so I sat on the one I had and got out my tobacco to think about it."

" 'What are y' doin'?' yells Huey.

" 'Rolling meself a smoke,' I says.

" 'It might be an idea to roll your smokes at night in future,' he says. 'I'm not paying a man to sit on his backside with his tobacco in his hand half the time. When I want a smoke-roller I'll employ one.'

"After about an hour I was getting the hang of it and Huey wandered off up the hill somewhere and left me to it. Next thing there was a hell of an explosion and hunks of dirt and wood flew all over the paddock. The horses must have been used to it because they didn't bolt; but I did!

" 'What are y' doin'?' yells Huey from up the hill.

" 'Getting out of the road,' I yells back.

" 'Well you won't get out of it that way,' he yells. And another one went up about twenty yards in front of me. The blast and a hunk of flying wood just about bowled me.

" 'Might be an idea to stay on the job,' yells Huey. 'I'll let you know if there's anything going up near you.'

"It was getting too dark to see where we were going by the time Huey decided to knock off. He told me to take the horses down to the harness-shed and feed them and put them out in the paddock, while he went up to the house to put a feed on.

" 'And don't get the collars and bridles mixed up,' he yells after me.

"I knew I might have a bit of trouble getting everything in the right place next morning so as I dropped the chains and unharnessed the horses I drew notes and diagrams in a patch of dirt under a macrocarpa. I fed the nags, hung all the harness in the shed and went up to the house.

"We had one big spud, two chops that looked as if they came off a rabbit and two slices of bread between us.

" 'Got any more tucker, mate?' I asked him when I'd finished.

" 'Yeah,' he says, 'but we'll have to save it for breakfast. Have to cut down a bit now there's two of us to feed. Not a millionaire, y' know.'

"I was starting to get a bit hot on old Huey by this time so I went to bed early to save blowing me top on him.

"Next morning, about an hour and a half before daylight, there was a hell of a crash on the roof of my fowl-house; Huey was up at the house throwing rocks to wake me up. We had a cold spud, two slices of bacon-fat and two pieces of bread between us for breakfast. He poured hot water out of the tap into last night's tea billy and had the hide to call it a brew.

"It was still dark when I went to get the horses and I couldn't see my diagrams in the dust. I struck a match and found that something had slept there anyway; I think it must have been one of the horses. Huey came down about an hour later and found me with a hell of a mess. I had the wrong collar on the wrong horse and I was trying to put it in the middle when it belonged on the other side at the back.

" 'What are y' doin'?' yells Huey.

" 'What's wrong?' I says.

" 'For a start,' he says, 'you've got that horse's hames on back to front, and that's not where she goes.'

" 'Might be an idea if you hook 'em up yourself,' I says.

" 'Might be an idea if you hit the track again,' he says.

" 'Might be an idea if you pay me for a day's work,' I says.

" 'Might be an idea if you take a runnin' jump at yourself,' he says.

"So, Jack me boy, being a peaceable sort of a bloke, even in them days, I shoulders my swag and slopes off. The job wasn't worth having, anyway."

Sam reached over and pinched out the candle and the last sounds Jack heard before he went to sleep were the cry of an owl and the distant croaking of frogs in the swamp down by the slips or skids, or whatever that ramp where they load the logs on to trucks was.

"My mate fell off a jigger-board a couple of weeks back," Sam said to Mr Hartshorne next morning. "Knocked his shoulder around a bit. Don't want him doing too much just yet to give it a chance to come right."

"That's the idea," agreed Mr Hartshorne. "You take it easy for a few days, lad. We don't want to make a cot-case out of you."

During the next few weeks Jack learned about scarfing, backing, limbing, deeing, sniping, jigger-boards, platforms, toms, strops, drives, triggers, and saw and axe sharpening. He learned that tawa splits out on you if you don't watch it, and broken-off branches — sailors — can fly fifty yards when a tree comes down, and bowl a man stone stinkin' dead if he's not careful.

They got into the habit of getting up to the bush just after daylight and knocking off in the middle of the afternoon so they could do a bit of washing or reading or tinkering around with the truck. Then the old chap who ran the cookhouse, a cantankerous old boy who'd been a cook at a boys' school for a few years before coming out to the bush, started complaining about them asking for feeds at odd hours of the day and night. Sam and he argued about every time they saw each other until one morning Sam and Jack arrived at the cookhouse for breakfast to find the door locked and a note hung on a nail informing them that breakfast would be available from 7.30 a.m. until 8.

Sam stood thoughtfully reading the note for a few minutes and then said: "Jack me boy, old Bill needs a bit of a wake-up. The trouble with these cooks is they think they can run the place. I think we'll just put one across him. He won't get much sympathy from the boss. I don't think Dan likes him any more than we do."

Jack was all for the idea of putting one across old Bill, who had been treating him, and feeding him, like a little boy. "I'm a starter, Sam," he said eagerly. "Let's rig up a bag of soot on the door for him."

"No," said Sam. "Something a little tougher on him than that."

"Drop a handful of cartridges in his fire," suggested Jack.

"No. He'd forget that too quick," said Sam. "Let's see now."

"What about sticking a horse in his hut?" said Jack. "A dead one," he added.

"Not a bad scheme, Jack, but we might get caught and that'd ruin everything."

"Eels in his bed?"

"No, same trouble. Hang on, Jack. I think I've got it. Follow me."

He led the way down to a dump by the skids, where they'd been splitting the short ends of logs into posts and strainers on the days when it was too wet or windy to work in the bush. Taking an end each of the biggest strainer they could find there they carried it back to the cookhouse. It was just breaking daylight.

"Righto, Jack," said Sam. "Put your end quietly down by the step there. Right in the middle. Now, I'll just lean this end against the door, like this, and we'll take off."

"But what's that for?" asked Jack.

"What's it for? Jack me boy, at exactly seven-thirty old Bill's going to open up his cookhouse and cop the end of that strainer fair in the bread-basket."

Jack was horrified. "But Sam," he said, "he might get hurt."

"That's the general idea, Jack me boy. Just to remind him he's not dealing with a bunch of brats at the Grammar School any more. Now let's clear out of here before he wakes up."

They had a cup of tea in their hut and went up to the bush where they selected a big silver birch as their second victim of the day. Jack was still worried about the idea of that strainer falling on the cook when he opened the door, but Sam didn't appear to be in the least concerned. He joked and chuckled about it as he cut notches for jigger-boards, while Jack cleared a space in the undergrowth to work in.

At nine o'clock the tractor-driver, a quiet bloke called Clive who kept strictly to himself, arrived and told Sam and Jack that they were wanted down at the boss's hut.

"How's old Bill this morning, Clive?" grinned Sam.

"He's okay," said Clive, "but Dan's not too good. In a bad mood about something."

"I suppose we'll have to amble down and cheer him up," said Sam resignedly. "Coming, Jack?"

They dug their axes into a handy stump and trudged off down the snigging-track.

"Do you think it's anything to do with that strainer, Sam?" asked Jack.

"Damn right it is," answered Sam. "Old Bill's probably been doing a bit of a moan to the boss about it. But don't worry about it, Jack me boy. I'm a better liar than that retired burglar of a cook ever looked like being."

"You there, Dan?" called Sam cheerfully, knocking loudly on the door of the office hut.

"Come in," said Dan Hartshorne quietly.

"Sit down, boys." And Sam and Jack sat on a bench that was so low they had to squint up at the boss, who towered above them across his desk. Jack started to shiver a little.

"Which one of you was it?" asked Dan.

"Was what?" asked Sam innocently.

"Was the dopey, half-witted fool who stuck the strainer against the cookhouse door this morning!" roared Dan suddenly.

Jack's head jerked back and struck the window-ledge. His eyes filled with tears and he wanted to blow his nose but Sam had their

42

only handkerchief. Sam reached into his hip pocket for the tobacco and began rolling a smoke.

"We wanted to give the cook a bit of a fright," he said. "He refuses to give us a feed before we go to work."

And Sam explained how he and Jack liked to get on the job at daylight so as to get in a decent day's work; but a man working as hard as they were couldn't be expected to keep going without a feed under his belt.

"Okay," said Dan, when Sam was finished. "One more stunt like that and you can pack your swag, the pair of you. Now you'd better go and get yourselves something to eat. You can take the strainer back to the dump when you go up to the job."

"Did we get 'im, boss?" asked Sam.

"No, you blasted idiots," bellowed Dan. "You got me! Now get out of here before I lay into you with your own strainer!"

Jack ducked out the door on Sam's heels, tripped on the doorstep and sprawled in the dust.

"Wonder what the hell went wrong," said Sam when they were out of earshot of the boss's hut.

"Everything," said Jack shakily.

Not a word was spoken as they got their breakfast off old Bill, who smirked and whistled out of tune while they ate. As they passed their plates back Sam said quietly to Bill: "We'll get you, Billy boy," and walked out after Jack. Jack wasn't interested in getting anyone just then.

As they carried the strainer back to the skids, Sam and Jack heard Dan Hartshorne roaring for the cook. That night a very subdued Bill told them to let him know what time they wanted breakfast in the morning.

Two days later Sam pointed out to Jack that the cookhouse door opened outwards instead of inwards as they'd thought. They later learned that the boss had been passing the cookhouse, noticed the strainer leaning on the door and called out for old Bill to open up. Bill, thinking there'd been an accident or something, had come charging out and shoved the strainer over into Dan's chest.

"The bloke who put that door on inside out should have got the blame," announced Sam indignantly, under his breath.

43

By the time Sam and Jack had been six weeks on the job they were putting out more logs than the tractor could handle, and Mr Hartshorne joked that they were sending him broke with all the money they were making. Jack took his first cheque, fifty-six pounds worth, in a blistered hand, and said, Ta, in the same careless way as Sam. He folded it in half, shoved it into his hip pocket, and dug his axe into a small tree that was in the way of the tractor. Mr Hartshorne, notebook in hand, was sitting on one end of a log, when Jack's tree fell back across it. Mr Hartshorne's end of the log shot six feet into the air, and Mr Hartshorne shot out into the gully.

The tractor-driver said: "Hell!"

Sam said: "Ta-ta!" and waved.

"Look out!" yelled Jack.

There was a brief interval of silence, while Mr Hartshorne struggled up through the crown-fern.

"You blundering, useless, bloody mongrel!" he roared. "If ever I saw a more ignorant, dopey fool of a miserable, bungling rat-bag . . ."

"Now just you hang on there a minute, mate!" said Sam, stepping forward. "You can't go talking to a mate of mine like that. You expect a man to work in your godforsaken lousy patch of scrub, where the rocks float and wood won't, and every tree leans a different way and hangs up and twists and splits and breaks off! And you start abusin' 'im when one of the blasted things falls back on 'im!"

"Get out! Get out! Get to hell out of here before I flatten the pair of you!" yelled Mr Hartshorne, waving a gigantic paw in Sam's face. "You're finished! Pack your gear and clear out!"

Just then he turned and caught the tractor-driver grinning. "What the hell are you laughing at, Murdoch?"

"Nothing — nothing, Mister Hartshorne," gulped the driver.

"Well get back to your job while you've still got one!"

"A hard man," said Sam, as they spluttered down the pumice road with a mixture of petrol and diesel-oil in the tank. "Just as well we got paid before that happened. A hard man. No sense of humour."

"Sorry about causing the trouble, Sam," said Jack. "I should

44

have left the thing alone in the first place."

"Don't let it worry you, Jack. We've got a hundred and twelve quid in our kick, and a hundred jobs that need two experienced men like us. It's time we were moving on anyway. I was going to suggest it myself once we got paid. By the way, always make your back-cut a bit higher than the scarf and leave plenty of wood so if she leans back you can wedge her over.

"Ah — here's the main road. Which way, Jack?"

A Bunch of Brumbies

Jack came to the door of the hut and yawned at the rain. It was three days since they'd moved into this old shanty on the edge of the plains to grapple with a few nags, as Sam had put it, and they'd done nothing but burn wood in the big tin fireplace and sort out the ropes and breaking-in gear for the wild horses they were going to catch and break in at tremendous profit. The two saddle-scarred and wind-broken hacks that Sam had bought from a Maori farmer stood with their rumps towards the blunt line of bush that showed dimly through the slanting rain. Jack wondered how they were ever going to catch wild horses with them. It sounded pretty good when Sam talked about it, but his idea of a lasso — inch and a half rope with big knots in it! And those patched-up old military saddles . . .

"Shut the door will you, Jack," called Sam from his bunk. "We can't have sunshine but at least we can keep ourselves warm. Throw another log on the fire and I'll show you how we used to bake bread in a billy when I was prospecting on the coast."

"Gold prospecting?"

"Too right. Would have made a fortune but for one little thing."

"What was that?"

"No gold. Now pass me pants and I'll whack up a loaf that your mother'd be proud of."

"Anything to do today, Sam?"

"Yep — wait till tomorrow and hope this rain lets up."

"I hope our horses are getting plenty to eat out there. Do you think they'll be fast enough to catch brumbies? I've never ridden over country like this before."

"It's not the horse or the way you ride it in this game, Jack me boy — it's where you ride it. Where did you put that bag of flour?"

In the early afternoon they were drinking tea and eating Sam's bread. Jack didn't like the taste of it much, but he told Sam it was pretty good. "Where did you learn horse-breaking, Sam?"

"Old bloke in the Hawke's Bay taught me. He could just about train a horse to cut firewood, old Andy Dunn. But when it came to anything apart from horses he was absolutely stonkered. Remember once Andy reckoned he was turning his old mare out the back for the winter because every time he went down to the pub in his buckboard . . ."

"A buckboard?"

"Yep, a real old buckboard. In pretty good nick it was, too. Just like the ones they used on the mail-runs in the old days. Andy made 'er up out of bits and pieces he picked up here and there. Used it for years.

"Well, as I was saying, Andy reckoned it wasn't safe to go down to the pub in the buckboard any more because every time he staggered out to drive home someone had unharnessed his old mare, poked the gig shafts through the gate and hooked the horse up on the other side. With the horse on one side of the gate and the buckboard on the other, old Andy mad as a gum-digger's dog, and everyone shouting advice and saying it wasn't them who done it, old Andy got fed up.

"He turned the mare out and ordered a brand-new pushbike. I'll never forget the day it arrived on the mail-truck, all black and shiny with paper round the frame and Andy's name on a big card. He wheeled her down to the shed where he kept all his gear and got out his tin of axle-grease. He reckoned the paper was to save it getting knocked around and wouldn't hear of us giving him a hand to take it off. He plastered grease all over himself and his new bike and wheeled it up to the road, turned her down the hill, got on the saddle and lifted his feet off the ground. He hit the bottom of the hill doing about forty and ploughed through our ducks that were sitting on the bridge, yelling 'Whoa there! Whoa!' to the bike. Killed one of the drakes stone dead and piled up in the fence by our gate.

"Next morning I heard him telling my mother it was just a young bike and would probably come right with a bit of careful handling. For a couple of weeks Andy wheeled that bike all over the farm with him to get it used to being handled."

"Did he ever get to ride it?" asked Jack, laughing.

"No, Jack me boy, old Andy finished up bringing in the old mare and sticking to his buckboard."

"What happened to the bike?"

"The bike got him beat the day he wheeled it four mile down to the pub and tied it to the fence alongside the horses. While he was in having a quiet beer, somebody unbolted the gate, threaded the rails through the bike frame and bolted it together again. Poor old Andy couldn't work that one out at all. Far as I know it's still there, wheeling back and forth every time the gate gets opened and shut. No, Andy wasn't exactly what you'd call brilliant, but when it came to handling a horse he couldn't be beat."

"Could he make old horses run fast?" asked Jack.

"I reckon Andy could have made a horse fly if he'd wanted to," replied Sam " — hey, it's stopped raining! Catch your horse and saddle up, Jack. We'll have a look round the place before it gets dark. Looks like we're in for a fine day tomorrow."

They rode along the bush-edge to where long tussock clearings fingered up the gullies into tall manuka. A small bunch of brumbies with a whistling, snorting stallion parading in the rear cantered up a shallow gut and threaded into the scrub. To Jack they looked magnificent, sweeping through the tussock, but Sam said they were a weedy mob of in-bred mongrels, so Jack said, "Yeah, they are, aren't they."

They rode up to where the horses had entered the scrub and Sam got off to have a look at the track.

They saw two more bands of brumbies before dark. The last one had about thirty assorted horses in the charge of a big chestnut stallion with a cream mane and tail. Sam conceded that there were one or two decent ones among them but they'd be lucky to get any of them because there were so many old skinny mares about. Riding back to the hut in the dark, Sam said that they were certain to get a few horses but most of them would be too old or just plain no-good and have to be let go again.

It took them a whole day to find a suitable place for their yard and a week to build it. In a clump of scattered trees roughly thirty yards wide and separated from the bush-edge by a shallow swamp, they built a fence with poles dragged across from the

51

bush. They stapled wire round the poles and on to trees a foot apart to a height of ten feet. It was an odd-shaped affair of three sections, with a tree in the middle of each for a snubbing-post, sliprails at one end, and a chute opening out into the swamp at the other.

"I'd sure hate Andy Dunn to see this," said Sam, as he hammered an extra staple into the last sliprail loop. "But I guess it'll do the job."

That evening Sam shot two deer along the bush-edge with some special cartridges he'd made for his old shotgun by mixing candle-grease with the lead shot to weld it into a solid ball. They packed all the meat back to the hut and hung it up "to ripen", as Sam put it.

"This stuff's no good to eat till she glows in the dark," he explained.

Sam had spent one of the wet days splicing eyes into the ends of twenty lengths of rope and after the evening meal he shook out one of the snares and said, "Gather round, Jack me boy. Here's how we're going to catch ourselves some of those long-haired, tussock-eating ngatis. First thing in the morning we'll ride quietly along to those tussock flats that run back into the scrub. The brumbies are used to us coming and going along there now, so it shouldn't be hard to cut them off. If they spot you and run for cover, let them go. If we try to head them off we'll never see them again. I'll come with you as far as the first run and carry on to the far mob. Now there's three main tracks in the first run. Go up them till you find a good strong tree. If you can't find one thick enough, two smaller ones growing close together will do. Loop this end of your rope round the tree and pull it tight. Then you make a noose out of the other end and hang it across the track on the scrub. Don't wedge it in anything and never have the top of your noose higher than this — " he dug Jack in the ribs with his finger. "When you get it set up lay a ducking-stick across the track at the top of your noose so the horse will duck his head under it and through the rope. Arrange the manuka to hide as much of the rope as possible and have it so it can't drop on to the ground when you shake the scrub around it. Got that?"

"Yeah, that's simple enough. What's this knot for?"

"That's to stop the noose pulling too tight and choking the horse. That's all there is to it; but don't forget — don't chase them if they run the wrong way. We can have another go on Friday if we miss them tomorrow."

That night Jack dreamt he was flying through the tussock leading the brumbies on a big chestnut stallion with a cream mane and tail until Sam shouted in the wind that stallions always tail the mob.

It was going to be a hot day but the dawn was as cold as an axe-head. Sam and Jack talked in whispers as they walked their horses slowly along the bush-edge to where the scrub started.

"Meet you by the dead matai," said Sam as they parted.

Jack took three of his snares, set them carefully on the tracks, and moved along to the next gut, where he set another two. Beyond this point there were so many tracks he had to guess which ones to snare. Sunlight was pouring over the plains by the time he reached the dead matai, where he waited half an hour for Sam.

"How did you get on, Jack?"

"Okay. I saw one mob out on the tussock from that rise back there."

"Good. I don't know where the big mob is. They might have gone back into the scrub, but I set eight snares anyway. We'll go back towards the hut and start on the bunch up that end and work this way. We might catch the big lot by that time."

The brumby mob was still out on the plain. They milled uncertainly as Sam and Jack rode towards them.

"Don't try and chase them into the scrub," said Sam. "Let them think they're doubling back past us. Once they're heading up the gut keep 'em moving. We want them to hit those tracks running. Right. Let 'er rip!"

They cantered towards the mob, and Jack felt the warm wind and the drumming of his excited horse's hooves on the tussock, and saw the high-headed, tail-sweeping wild horses race past in a graceful thundering stream. They ran them up the narrowing strip of tussock to the far end, and saw them suddenly scatter through the scrub as two hit the snares and plunged in frantic, snorting circles, trying to free themselves.

"Don't go too close to them, Jack!" yelled Sam. "We'll sneak up and have a look at what we've got."

The first was a rough-coated, stocky little mare with a wild mane and a wilder eye. The other was an old mare that was already weakening in her attempts to pull free.

"We'll cut the old girl loose when we get back," said Sam. "The other'll make a good little hack by the time we're finished with her."

They found the other two mobs and got seven of them in the snares. Four were suitable for breaking in.

"That's the best haul I've seen yet," said Sam happily. "We'll clean up close on a hundred quid with this lot."

When they arrived back at the first two horses they were standing quietly but the men's approach set them struggling again. Sam rode up and cut the old mare loose. Then he threw a loop over the other's head and pulled her out to the end of the snare.

"Take that end off the tree and keep it tight, Jack," he said. "She can't get near you while I've got this end. Keep your horse steady and we'll ease her out into the open."

With surprisingly little trouble they got the brumby down to the tussock and led her across to the yard. Herding her into the small pen at the end, they returned for the next one, a Roman-nosed bay that Sam called Caesar and reckoned would make a good stock-horse.

By the middle of the following day Sam and Jack had five partially-subdued brumbies in their pens. In four days they would all tie and lead in various measures of docility, depending on how quickly they'd realised the futility of trying to break away from the snubbing-posts. With only two sets of mouthing gear it was over a week before all the horses were mouthed and answering to the reins.

The little mare they had caught first was named Amber. She was very easy to handle. By the time Sam was ready to start riding them she would come to the rails and eat out of Jack's hand. They led her into the chute first and blindfolded her. Then Sam gently put his saddle on her and girthed it tight. Jack was mounted on one of the hacks with a long rope on to Amber's bridle.

"If she throws me," said Sam, "hang on to that rope for all you're worth. We don't want her getting away with our best saddle."

Sam climbed into the saddle and Jack drew the bars on the end of the chute and whipped off Amber's blindfold. She stood there for a moment and then jumped forward into the swamp. Hock-deep in water and mud she could do no more than plunge and flounder. When she quietened down, Sam eased her gently on to firm ground. They cantered along the plain for a few hundred yards and then steadied to a trot.

"There you are, Jack me boy," said Sam, patting the mare's sweaty neck. "She's all yours. You'll have to take her very easy for a few days but she'll make a nice little hack. One of the freest moving horses I've seen for a long time."

Caesar ploughed straight through the swamp and bucked Sam off on the other side. They put her back in the chute for another go. This time she reared up and fell over sideways in the mud. Sam got his leg from underneath just in time.

"Take her round again, Jack. If we don't best her this time we'll have no end of trouble with her."

The third try was successful and Sam gave the horse a long run across the plains.

"That'll do for us today, I think," Sam said, turning Caesar into the yard. "We'll ride another couple tomorrow and give these two another go. Should have them finished in a week or ten days."

"What are we going to do then?" asked Jack.

"We'll have to take the horses to a sale or a sheep-station to sell them. Then we can cruise round for a bit till we have to get another job."

HARVEY WILSON'S RUN

Sam went on ahead in the truck to strike a deal with the Maori farmer they'd bought the hacks from. Jack rode Amber and led the other five horses in a chain behind him.

When he reached the Maori's farm he found Sam arguing hopelessly that the hacks were in better shape than when they'd bought them. With time against him, for they had to reach Paranui station before nightfall, he'd dropped from two quid up and was back to the purchase price. Ten minutes later the Maori handed over half the original price and had the decency to grin broadly and offer them a feed as he did so.

They arrived at the Paranui homestead in the late afternoon. Sam asked for the owner and they shook hands with a short, plump man who looked at their horses and said he didn't know whether he could use all of them.

"Tell you what, though," he said. "One of my musterers is leaving tomorrow to go droving with his brother. He asked me to keep my eye open for a good stock-horse. Why don't you chaps stay the night and see him when he comes in from the back in the morning? It'll give me a chance to think about those horses."

"Thanks," said Sam. "We'll do that. Our time's our own."

"You chaps not working?" asked the station owner.

"No. We've just finished breaking in this bunch of nags."

"I'm short of a couple of musterers, if you're interested. Done any sheep work before?"

"Sheep work, he says!" cried Sam, turning and winking at Jack. "Have you ever heard of Harvey Wilson's block down south, boss?"

"Can't say I have, offhand. The name sounds familiar though."

"Well, Harvey Wilson's got the toughest sheep-run in the country." quoted Sam. "Homestead's at three and a half thousand feet and you can't get a horse over three-quarters of the place. What isn't vertical is overhanging. We had to muster it off on foot and they lost more dogs there every year than any other part of the country. They fall off the hillsides."

"Cripes, they must lose a lot of stock in a place like that! There's nothing near as bad up this way," said the boss.

"No offence, boss, but down on Harvey Wilson's run we used to call country like this flats. I'd hate to think what the boys would say if they found out we were working here. Probably laugh us off the station."

"Well, think it over, boys, and let me know tomorrow. You can put your horses in the ram paddock for tonight and use the far end of the shearers' quarters. You'll have to kid to old Charlie down at the cookhouse a bit; but his bark's worse than his bite and he puts a good feed in front of you. Take an armful of firewood each as you go in and he's your friend for life."

They closed the gate on their horses and walked round the woolshed and down towards the cookhouse.

"It looks to me," said Sam, "as though the boss is going to buy our horses, providing we stay and work for him. He's a shrewd man."

"But I can't muster sheep," said Jack, alarmed.

"Yes, you can, Jack me boy. There's nothing in it. I'll fill you in on a few of the details tonight. We'll have to pick up two or three dogs each but that won't be hard in a place like this. Anything that makes plenty of noise and comes when you call it will do to get by with."

Next morning they sold one of their horses to the departing musterer for a tenner and two huntaway pups that he said were just coming right. Jack bought the cook's old cattle dog for two quid and Sam got the cowman-gardener's beardie to train for him "like we handle 'em down south".

"You won't know him for the same dog when you get him back," said Sam, patting the slightly overwhelmed old chap on the shoulder.

Then to Jack: "We'll hang on to Amber and Caesar for hacks and sell the other one to the boss for fifteen quid. That'll give us twenty-five quid and we'll still have a good horse each. How does that sound?"

"Perfect," said Jack. "Do you think he'll give us that much for it?"

"Course he will," said Sam. "If he doesn't pay it, he won't get his two experienced musterers."

"Yes, I think that'll be all right," said the boss, when Sam told him they were ready to start work. "Do you want the cheque now?"

"You can leave it till you pay us off, if you like," said Sam. "We won't be needing any money while we're here."

"Righto. You'll be on the usual two pounds a day and keep. Er — isn't that old Charlie's Nigger you've got there?"

"That's him," said Sam. "We're going to make a dog out of him."

"I don't know that you'll get much work out of that old scrap-eater," said the boss doubtfully.

"Boss," said Sam, as though he was disclosing for the first time a never-failing cure for facial eczema, "I once heard it told how Harvey Wilson drove a swarm of bees from Nelson to Kaikoura with two of his dogs, without losing a single bee. And he used to say that it was better to have a crook dog in the hands of a good man than to have good dogs in the hands of a bad one — I don't reckon there's much anyone could tell old Harvey about running a station."

"Yes, I suppose you've got something there," chuckled the boss. "But I certainly hope you don't have any trouble with old Nigger. Charlie could never do a thing with him except feed him. The packman-cook is due in for supplies tomorrow so you can go back out with him. We're starting the shearing muster in a few days."

That afternoon Sam put their first sets of shoes on Amber and Caesar. Caesar's hind legs had to be roped up.

The packman-cook was a muttering-to-himself old man called Joe, who took no notice of anybody and spoke, when he spoke, in the same grumpy tone that he used to the boss himself. Sam and Jack gave him a hand to load the boxes and bags of supplies on to four pack-horses; but Joe checked everything they did to make sure it was right. Jack saw him unbuckle a surcingle Sam had tightened and do it up again in the same hole.

Joe rode off in the lead and his pack-horses fell into their places behind him. Sam and Jack followed behind and the whole procession was strung out over a hundred yards of the track, which led up a low tussocky ridge from the homestead and then zigzagged down into a wide valley on the other side. Away ahead, beyond the last grey ridge of tussock and scrub, Jack could see a dark, snow-topped range of mountains and wondered how close to them they were going. He decided to ask Joe the next time he passed him on one of the zigzags but, when he did, there was no reply and Jack could have sworn the old man's eyes were closed.

"Do you think we'll be anywhere near those mountains with the snow on them, Sam?" he asked.

"Probably be working right in them," replied Sam.

"But we'd never get that far in one day!"

"You'd be surprised, Jack me boy. Distances are very deceptive in this sort of country. You can travel all day towards a landmark and never seem to get any closer. Then, bang, you're suddenly there. Something to do with the dead ground, I s'pose."

"Dead ground?"

"Yeah, dead ground is the country in hollows and between ridges that you can't see when you're looking at something a long way off, like those mountains there — get in behind there, Nigger! We'll have to bring that dog under control, Jack. Slinky looking mongrel, isn't he. Reminds me of a dog a neighbour of ours had when I was a kid. Cost him his farm in the end and sent him off his rocker."

"Yeah'? How the hell did that happen?" asked Jack incredulously.

"It all started when Henry — that's the bloke whose dog it was — broke off his engagement to the local postmistress and got this dog off an old Dally scrub-cutter. For three days and nights the dog had been howling and hollering so you could hear it all over the district. People started going crook about the noise so the Dally offered the dog to Henry to see if he could do anything with it. The postmistress, who hated dogs, told Henry she wasn't going to have anything to do with him any more if he took it; but Henry took it just the same.

"The dog quietened down as soon as Henry took it home and a couple of days later they found the Dally dead on the hillside. He'd fallen across his slasher and bled to death. Used to take fits or something, I believe.

"After that you never saw Henry without the dog was sloping along beside him. Nobody ever saw him tie it up or work it or anything. Just used to take it everywhere he went. It'd even wait outside the pub when he went in for a beer and watch at the door till he came out.

"Then, nobody knew how it got started but a rumour went round that the dog howling had had something to do with the old Dally bloke getting killed. All the women believed it and all the men reckoned it was a lot of tripe.

"Bert Mildon reckoned Henry hadn't paid for the dog and was scared someone would swipe it if he left it tied up. Don Mildon said Henry's dog was something to do with the postmistress. Percy Singer's mother-in-law told my mother we ought to put an end to all this disgraceful gossiping and nonsense; but if we asked her Henry had an arrangement with the Devil, who'd put the dog there to keep an eye on him. That was about the time Henry was the only one who planted beans and that year there was a shortage of them. Everyone else had gone in for pumpkins, and they weren't worth taking in to the market. Then Digger Watson's wife had a vision of Henry lying dead by the big corner pool in the creek with the dog feeding off him and smoke all over the place. Uncle Wally used to spit on the ground and say Henry was too miserable to shout himself a collar and chain.

"Henry went about his work same as ever, but he must have noticed how everyone was talking about him and looked when he went past. And then Missus Rogers at the store told him he'd get no more stuff from her if he let that dog in her shop, where respectable people got their things. Henry used to get his groceries at the door after that and Missus Fletcher said how the dog had Henry in its power and all the mothers told us kids not to talk to him, or even raid his orchard, because something terrible might happen if we did.

"Then one night the dog started howling on the hill above Henry's place and howled every night for nearly a week. People started saying it looked as if Henry was going to go the same way as the old Dally.

"On Sunday the Reverend — I forget his name now — gave a

63

sermon about breaking free from the clutches of the Devil. Henry was at church and the dog waited outside — probably heard every word of it. Afterwards they walked straight off, Henry moving slow and sad, and the dog slinking along same as ever.

"Next morning the pair of them came past our place, heading for the railway station with a couple of suitcases. All the talking about him and his dog had got too much for him I reckon. Everyone went over when they auctioned off his farm and gear because there might be stuff going cheap."

"What rotten people!" cried Jack indignantly. "All that stink over an ordinary bloke and his dog."

"I'm not so sure about that part of it," said Sam. "You see, when they tried to put the dog in a box in the guard's van it went berko and attacked the stationmaster. Then it clouted down on Henry's wrist and they had to work its jaws open with a track-lever. Then it bit everyone it could get its teeth into.

"They locked it in the ticket office in the finish and the police came and shot it. Heard the five shots from up at our place. One of the blokes who was there said the dog must have got so scared, being separated from Henry, that it went completely crazy — bloodshot eyes, foaming mouth, snarling and biting. He wouldn't talk about it in front of the kids in case of nightmares.

"We never saw Henry again but somehow it got round that he'd finished up in the nut-house. And that dog was the dead spitting image of old Nigger here. Good thing we've got the old shotgun with us. We can knock him off if he gets out of control."

Jack watched Nigger very closely for signs of abnormal behaviour for a while after Sam had finished his tale, but he acted as normal as any other lazy, useless dog. By this time they had reached the river and Joe's horses were plodding steadily upstream.

"Must be going to follow the river-bed for a while," observed Sam. "Watch your horse on the crossings, Jack. They're not used to the water. Might have to get off and lead them across the first time or two."

With a bit of coaxing and snorting Amber splashed nervously over the first belly-deep crossing behind the pack-horses. Caesar followed for a few yards and then wheeled and plunged straight downstream into a deep hole. Sam dragged her head round and swam her back up against the current until she could climb out into the shallows again. Then he spurred her across the last twenty yards at a canter.

No sooner had they crossed the river than they had to cross back again. This time Caesar only pranced a bit and Amber crossed quietly enough.

"Looks as though they'll be getting plenty of river work before we get there, eh Jack?" remarked Sam.

"Yeah, I suppose there's miles of this yet."

"You measure distance in country like this by the number of hours it takes to travel from one place to another," explained Sam. "But you're probably right. We'll see a few hours of the river all right."

The evening was beginning to chill the mountain air when Joe turned off on a track that left the river where it forked into two steep streams. They wound up towards a rough line of bush that was blotted across the foothills of the range Jack had thought they would never reach. He shifted stiffly in the saddle and realised he had never ridden so far at one time in his life before — or felt so hungry.

"Should be there in an hour or so," said Sam. But it was two hours and getting dark by the time a shaft of smoke coming from a clump of beech trees in a gully and the barking of dogs greeted their arrival. The dogs seemed to be tied to every clump of tussock within a hundred yards of the hut.

"Don't forget to give your horse a good rub-down, Jack," said Sam, dropping his saddle to the ground. "That looks like the horse paddock down there."

Two men came out of the hut and helped Joe unload the pack-horses. One of them, Jack noticed, was only a year or two older than he was.

"G'day," said Sam. "I'm Sam and this is Jack. We've come to do the muster with you blokes."

There were six other musterers altogether and, after being introduced all round, Jack tried to remember their names.

There was Brian, the young chap; Fred, the tall dark one; Tai, the little Maori bloke; Mac, with the hook nose and black teeth;

Nick, with the ginger beard; and Blue, with red hair, who was the head musterer. Blue was about thirty-five years old and had spent all his life in the back-country. He had a permanent squint, as though he was looking into the sun all the time, and his face was so brown and wrinkled you could easily have mistaken his age for about fifty. "Got a face on 'im like a handful of tobacco," as Sam described it later.

The hut was dark and smoky with ten bunks round the walls and an enormous fireplace. A camp-oven and three tin billies hung steaming over the fire. Sam and Jack threw their sleeping bags on spare bunks, put their mugs on the table with the others and fitted in with the gang right off. They seemed a pretty good bunch.

THE MUSTER

Jack woke, it seemed, a few moments after going to sleep, to find it was morning and everyone was drinking tea. He filled his mug from the billy and sat beside Sam on a bunk.

"I want you blokes to go round to the Snow Hut and hunt the sheep down into the valley from the open spur," said Blue. "Nick will go with you as far as Deer Clearing and point out the way."

"Sounds easy," said Sam, tossing the dregs of his tea into the fire. "You in any hurry for them?"

"No, you can take a week if you want to. We're only filling in time till we find out when the shearers are coming. Once you get all your sheep in the valley all you have to do is ride along once a day and hunt down the ones that try to get back to the high stuff. You'd better take a pack-horse with you. The rest of us will pick up your lot on the way through with the main mob."

Nick left them on a windswept ridge with some very vague sounding instructions. "Could you make out what he was talking about, Sam?" asked Jack, with a worried glance at Nick's distant back.

"Not too well," replied Sam, leading the way down a steep spur. But we'll find it all right. The pack-horse seems to know where he's going anyway."

They travelled across ridge after ridge and then picked their way along a boulder-strewn creek-bed. Sam pointed out several groups of deer high up on the ridges and once a bunch of big black pigs lumbered into the scrub ahead of them. Sam called the dogs in behind.

"Even if they do bail one we won't be able to shoot it," he said. "The horses'd be back on the plains before we knew where we were."

At the head of the creek they climbed into a low saddle and looked down into a rolling, heaping, staggering, sliding valley. Scattery bush spilled over the ridge tops and dribbled down the

69

gullies, where it dried up about halfway down. Great, grey shingle slides lay spread against the mountain-sides from top to bottom and sprinkled white specks of sheep dotted the tussock.

"Hut should be somewhere along this side of the valley to the left," said Sam. "We'll follow the pack-horse from here on and hope he doesn't put us crook."

They found the Snow Hut on a grassy ledge beside a patch of bush. The only level piece of ground in the horse paddock was a little swamp where the water-hole was. The hut was just a hut.

"Pretty rough," observed Sam, "but the scenery's fair enough."

"It's terrific," agreed Jack. "I'll light the fire while you unload the pack-horse, if you like."

"Righto. I reckon we've just about earned ourselves a brew of tea. I'll see if I can find the milk and sugar first."

After a couple of mugs of tea and a cigarette each, they took the dogs along the top of a ridge for a try-out. They found a bunch of sheep in a little hollow, and discovered that the cowman-gardener's beardie was something of a heading dog. The two huntaway pups hunted away and Nigger barked lazily when threatened with a stick. Sam carried on round the ridge with his shotgun to get a deer for meat and dog tucker, while Jack took the dogs back to the hut and cooked a feed. Sam came in after dark with the hindquarters of a stag across his shoulders.

"You can take the old musket and have a go next time if you like, Jack," he said. "You've got to sneak up real close to them before you shoot because after about forty yards the lead and candle-grease flies to bits and goes all over the place."

"Thanks, Sam. I'll have a crack tomorrow afternoon. We'll need plenty of meat for the dogs anyway. Might even get a pig if we're lucky and have pork chops for breakfast!"

Next morning they took a huntaway pup each and Sam took the beardie and Jack, Nigger. Jack's hobnails rang on the frost-tempered ground and he called, "Get in behind, you black mongrel!" to his dogs because that was what Sam did. He saw the flow of wool and bidi-bidi building up towards the bottom of the valley and felt pleased because he knew he was doing a good job and, if he was lucky, Sam might even tell a yarn after tea.

With Jack working along the top of the ridge and Sam halfway down the side they worked all the sheep off that side of the valley and down to the river in a day and a half. The other side was rougher and took them three days. After that all they had to do was see that none of the sheep went back up the valley, and wait for the others to bring the main mob through.

"Should we count the sheep we've mustered, Sam?" Jack asked on their way back to the hut on the afternoon they finished the valley.

"No. We'd never get an accurate count the way they are now," Sam said. "Wouldn't do any good anyhow once they're mixed up in the main mob." They reached the hut and, while he built up the fire and Jack peeled the potatoes, Sam continued, "Besides, it doesn't pay to be too good on the counting business. Bloke I know made over a thousand quid by not being able to count properly."

"Fair go?" said Jack.

"Yep. Old Mick. He never was much good at working things out properly. To begin with I remember once when we were cutting flax in the Manawatu . . ."

"Flax cutting, Sam?" said Jack, who had still not realised that Sam, once he was rolling, didn't need a shove.

"Yeah. Didn't last long on that job. Didn't hit it off too good with the foreman. He reckoned I couldn't cut cards and I said I wasn't too bad on throats, and he said to see how good I was at cuttin' across to the office and collecting me time. You can't win. Anyhow, old Mick had a knife he reckoned was twenty-eight year old. Four new blades and three new handles he'd put on 'er. I told him I'd had my slasher ever since it was a little wee pocket knife and what about cross-breeding them but Mick didn't see the joke. Couldn't convince him it wasn't the same knife he'd made out of a hunk of breaking-down saw when he was a young feller.

"Anyway, if he'd been able to count he'd still be putting up fences for two-ten a chain, instead of doing the Whenuaroa mail-run in a flash new truck.

"You see, Mick used to go to the races once a year. Never missed the autumn meeting at Trentham as long as I knew him. Well, last year, towards the end of March, he turns up at my place in a taxi and with a new suit on. Hardly recognised the old sod at first.

" 'Sam,' he says, 'I've made me pile!'

" 'What?' says I. 'Did you get yourself a post-hole digger at last?'

" 'No, Sam,' he says, 'I've got an unbeatable racing system. Look here!' and he shows me a thousand quid's worth of fivers he's got in his kick.

" 'Hell, Mick, you've done a bank over!' I says.

" 'No, Sam. I got it all off the races. A fiver's worth of the double at Trentham. You see, I bet in sevens. Can't miss.'

" 'How come?' says I.

" 'Nothing to it,' he says. 'I put me fiver on number seven in the first leg and she romps in. Number seven in the second leg was a bit of a mongrel so I looks up number fourteen. It was scratched, so I figured 'er out — three sevens — twenty-two. I put me dough on number twenty-two, and the next thing I'm round collecting the cash!'

"So you see, Jack me boy, education's not everything by a long shot."

In the cold mountain days, Jack learned how to sneak up on deer and shoot them with Sam's old shotgun and the candle grease cartridges. He learned how to bake a loaf of bread in the iron camp-oven, tickle trout in the creek, and how to guess whether it was going to rain or not by the way the cloud lay along the range in the mornings. In the cold mountain evenings Sam told him how in the big cities they work by hours and minutes and save their money to buy things they don't want because they've already got everything they need. And how they wear small shoes because they don't want anyone to know they've got big feet, and ladies are more important because of their sex and men have to let them go first through doors and things. How shop windows are for seeing what you look like in, and a job writing letters is more important than a job fixing fences, and you pay more for a leg of meat than a good knife. How flash cars are for paying off and insurance companies. And when you buy a house you still have to go on paying for it after it's paid for, because of rates and things. And if you don't watch it they'll get you for income tax and sock you a hundred quid right off.

Hundreds of things Jack learned off Sam in the days they loafed and waited until the big mob poured down the main valley in a rolling, surging cloud, soaked up Sam and Jack's mob and carried it along. The other musterers climbed the ridge to the hut for a boil-up, then the eight of them rode down to the river and set the big mob moving again. Sam and Jack were sent out to one side to watch for strays and keep the mob from spreading. Jack felt more important then than he'd ever felt before. He galloped back and forth shouting, "Speak up Moss!" and whistling Nigger to go and head off a straying sheep, then riding round it himself because Nigger took no notice of him and refused to leave the horse's heels. It was a waste of time trying to work Nigger but Jack worked him just the same because it sounded good.

They hunted the mob — Sam reckoned there were about sixteen thousand — down the valley past the Rimu Hut and then went back to it for the night. Joe had come on ahead and had a hot meal ready for them. Every man fed his dogs, tied them up and put his horse in the paddock before going in for a feed.

"Should have the mob down to the homestead by this time tomorrow," said Sam as he and Jack walked towards the hut after letting their horses go.

"What then?" asked Jack.

"I don't know, Jack. We could probably stay on here for a while but once a man's done a thing it's a waste of time doing it again. What say we get our dough and shove off?"

"Suits me, Sam," said Jack. "How much do you reckon we've got coming to us for this job?"

"Ah — let's see. Be about twenty-five quid each, besides what we get for the horse."

"What are we going to do with Amber and Caesar?"

"We'll have to get rid of them — that is unless you reckon we might need them. But we won't be able to get far with them and the truck too."

"Yeah, I suppose we'll have to see the boss about it."

"I think Nick might be interested in buying Amber. He was asking me about her today. Asked me if you wanted to sell her."

"I'll see him about it then. What about Caesar?"

"One of the others might take her. If not I'll have to go to work on the boss."

Next day they drove the mob into the paddock behind the homestead. Amber was knocked down to Nick for a tenner because that was all he could borrow off the others. Sam rode Caesar up to the homestead and came back to the cook-house an hour later with two cheques. One for two horses and the other for his and Jack's wages.

"He's a shrewd man," said Sam, winking at Jack. "Knocked me down from twenty-five quid to seventeen pound ten for Caesar."

Charlie and the cowman-gardener got their dogs back and Sam played cut-throat poker for the two huntaway pups with Tai and Fred and won three more. Then they all started swapping and Sam ended the evening with Fred's .303 rifle and four hundred rounds of ammunition. Jack got a hand-made knife and sheath and a copy of Banjo Paterson's poems off Brian for his pup.

While Sam took up a bit of slack in the truck's brake-rods next morning, Jack tightened up a loose petrol pipe connection. He forced it so tight that the pipe screwed off at the tank and petrol poured out all over the place. He had to stand there with his thumb over the hole while Sam searched the woolshed for something to plug it with. He finally carved a wooden plug and screwed it tightly into the hole.

"We'll have to stick a pipe in the top of the tank and set a siphon going to the carb," said Sam, after thinking for a while.

They took off the windscreen-wiper hose, which didn't work anyway, jammed one end on to the broken pipe, and twisted a wire tightly round the joint. The other end they poked into the tank and jammed it there with a chip of wood.

"It's a bit on the short side," said Sam. "But it'll do till we get where we're going. Wherever that is."

He got petrol running through the pipe and Jack started the motor. They drove the two miles out to the main road and stopped by a pool to fill the radiator.

"We've seen where this road comes from, Jack me boy," said Sam, as they climbed back in the cab. "Let's see where she goes to, shall we?" And they turned down a metalled road that

74

wandered wearily back and forth through endless clay cuttings and manuka-covered hills. The truck stopped by an old wooden bridge in a gully and they poured handfuls of stones into the tank to bring the petrol up to where the hose could reach it.

"Have a bo-peep at this little lot, Jack," called Sam from the back of the truck, where he was collecting stones. Jack went round and saw the cowman-gardener's beardie wagging his tail among their sacks and boxes of gear.

"If we take him back we'll run out of gas halfway and if we don't they'll think we swiped him," said Sam, scratching his head.

"We could write the old boy a letter from somewhere, saying what happened," suggested Jack.

"That's an idea now," agreed Sam. "We can say we'll send him back as soon as we get a chance. That'll put us in sweet with him. In the meantime he's ours. If we see any more of those goats along the road we'll bowl one for dog tucker."

It took Sam nine shots with his new rifle to knock a young nanny-goat off a hillside above the road.

"Couldn't hit a cow in the backside with a wet spade today," he complained, throwing two hind legs on to the truck. "You'd better have the next go, Jack."

Jack did have the next go a couple of miles farther on. After seven shots the goat he was shooting at walked lazily into the scrub.

"Let's try this thing out on a target," said Sam. "Looks to me as if she might be euchred."

They had turns at trying to hit a rock on a land-slip and their bullets all went several feet wide of the target.

"Barrel's had it all right," announced Sam. "Looks like we've been had, Jack me boy. We'll see if we can drop her off in a pub somewhere for a fiver. No flies on old Fred, eh!" They climbed into the truck laughing.

THE PAHAU VALLEY PUB

Their one headlight shone yellow, like an old dog's eye, on the only building Sam and Jack had seen since they'd left the Paranui station. The radiator was hissing like heavy rain and the petrol-tank was three-quarters full of stones . "Looks like a pub," said Sam.

"There's no lights on," yawned Jack. "What's the time, Sam?"

"Twenty to twelve. What say we camp here for the night and try and get some petrol from the pub in the morning?"

"Good idea. I've just about had it."

Jack got the sleeping bags out of Sam's pack while Sam lit a fire by a clump of manuka on the roadside. The ground was only a little harder than the bunks in the Snow Hut and they were more than tired enough to make up the difference.

Jack woke, starving hungry, in a bleak morning and a howling wind. A few heavy drops of rain tocked on to his sleeping bag. He shook Sam and they threw a cover over their dog and gear and sat in the truck, watching driven layers of rain knife across the scrubby hillsides.

"We'd better drive over to the pub and see if they're up yet," said Sam.

"I see a bit of smoke coming out of the chimney," said Jack. "Do you think we could get breakfast there?"

"We'll certainly have a go at it," replied Sam. "I could eat a horse and then have a lash at the harness!"

They stood in the rain that slanted under the veranda and hammered on a rattly front door.

"Wish they'd hurry up," said Sam. "Me legs are gettin' wet."

"Same here," said Jack. "Shall we try the back door?"

"Might be an idea. They must be deaf or something."

Sloshing their way around the side of the building, Jack saw a shadow of movement in a window as someone snatched themselves away from a gap in the curtain. Sam knocked loudly on the back door. No answer. Jack knocked; still no one came. They both knocked.

"Anyone home?" called Sam loudly, shaking the door handle and hammering on the wall.

"Let's get back to the truck," said Jack. "We're going to get soaked standing out here."

"They must be still in bed," said Sam, slamming the truck door. "We might as well wait for them to get up. There's obviously no show of getting petrol anywhere else round here."

"Perhaps they don't encourage visitors," said Jack. "I saw someone duck away from the window when we went round the side there."

"You sure?"

"Too right. Couldn't see much of them but there was smoke coming out of the chimney before. There's none now."

"Well, there's no doubt about it being a pub. It's a quarter to eight now; if they don't open up by nine we'll tear the place to bits."

"I don't see any sign saying it's a pub, Sam. There's only one 'Bar' on that window there."

"That'll be their sign lying in the grass over there," said Sam, pointing. "It's fallen down. We'll have a look at it when the rain eases off a bit.

"Y'know, this reminds me of a mate of mine whose wife locked him out of the house one night. Cold as wet scrub it was, and dark as all hell."

"What did he do about it?" asked Jack, passing Sam the tobacco and settling comfortably into his corner, with one muddy boot on the dashboard.

"Well, Tony Austin — that's this bloke's name — and I were working a block of pine bush up at Tokoroa and every weekend Tony used to whip off up to Hamilton to see a marvellous girl he spent all week talking about. A fortnight before he was due to get married I went droving down Stratford, but I got a letter from Tony a few months after he was hitched. He had a contract of his own and was making money hand over fist. He was paying off a section in Tokoroa and talking about putting in for one of them Government loans to build a house with. Everything was sweet.

"Three years after I'd last seen him I was passing through Putaruru and called in for a beer. There was Tony, leaning in his old place at the bar, drinking on his own. We had quite a fair little reunion, talking about old times and new times. He'd just finished building his house and Shirl — that's his wife — and their two boys were in good nick. A mate of Tony's, I forget his name, came in and by six o'clock we were going strong. We bought a crate each and Tony said to come down to his place for a feed. We pulled into the driveway of his flash house and he said: 'Hang on a tick, you blokes, I'll just nip in and tell Shirl you're coming.'

"Jack, me boy, you just wouldn't believe it! Me and this other bloke waited outside for half an hour — cleaned up two bottles each — while Tony and his missus argued about whether we were coming in or not.

"At last Tony came out and said to come in but not to stay long because Shirl wasn't feeling too good. Talk about embarrassing! We took a crate into his flash lounge — carpets and pictures on the walls and everything — and got stuck into it. Every now and again his missus would sing out from the kitchen: 'Don't spill beer on the carpet, Tony.' 'Don't put bottles on the new table, Tony.' 'How long are you going to be in there boozing, Tony?' and Tony just sat there saying: 'No dear; yes dear; no dear' all the time. She went to bed about ten o'clock telling him to come at once. Me and the other bloke offered to go but Tony said to stay, so we stayed.

"It turned into quite a decent little party after that. We brought another crate in and sat there telling yarns and remembering things that had happened and talking about things that should happen. Then we got hungry and Tony said a bloke he didn't like had a whole swag of overfed hens, so we got into his truck with a bottle each and went to get some. Lifted a couple of good'ns each and went back to Tony's.

" 'Hullo,' he said, 'here's a bottle on the ground. One of you blokes must have dropped it.' I picked it up and followed him to the front door. It was locked.

" 'Hey, there's bottles all over the lawn!' said the other bloke. And sure enough there were. Tony came back from trying the back door and said that it was locked too.

" 'Shirl must have thought we weren't coming back,' he said. 'I'll wake her up to let us in.' And he went and tapped softly on the bedroom window, saying: 'Shirl, Shirl, it's me, dear. I'm home.' Then the window flew open and caught him smack on the side of the head.

" 'You needn't think you're bringing your foul-mouthed, boozing mates into my house again,' she yelled at him. 'You can get out of it, all of you!'

" 'But Shirl . . .'

" 'Don't you but Shirl me. You're not coming in and that's final! Now get out, you're waking the kids up!'"

Sam paused to relight his smoke. "What happened then?" asked Jack.

"Well, Tony says to his old woman, sort of quiet: 'Mum, you've got ten seconds to open the front door.'

" 'How dare you talk to me like that! You needn't think you can come round here threatening me in my own home, you drunken bully!'

" 'Five seconds, Mum,' says Tony.

" 'You're drunk or you wouldn't dare say things like that.'

" 'You're sure you know what you're doing, Shirl? If you don't open the door I'm coming in just the same.'

"She slammed the window, yelling for him to wait till he was sober.

"Tony walked across to his truck, got a chainsaw off the back and started her up. Sounded like a full-grown motor-bike race. Then he went up and shoved her fair through the wall of his flash new Government-loan house. He ripped her down one side, across the top, down the other side and along the bottom. There was smoke and sparks and sawdust and noise all over the place. Never seen so much damage done so quickly in all me life. He carved a hole you could have driven this truck through and booted the whole section into his lounge with the carpets and pictures on the walls.

" 'Come on into my house, boys,' he said. 'Bring a few of those bottles. I'll send Mum out to pick up the rest in a minute.'"

"And did he?" asked Jack.

"Did he what?"

"Send her out for the rest of the beer?"

"Jack me boy, he not only sent her out for the beer but he made her pour it. Then he told her to go and get the chooks we'd lifted and pluck them in the flash Government-loan bath. She cooked us one of the best feeds I ever had in me life. And afterwards she sat beside her old man on the edge of the hunk of wall he'd pushed in and drank beer and joked and looked at him like he'd just saved her life. Never saw a woman change so much so quick in all me born days."

"What made her go like that?" cried Jack.

"I s'pose he *had* saved her life in a way," said Sam.

"But how?"

"Well, she might have been alive before but she certainly wasn't living, and she'd turned Tony into a sort of male house-keeper. Without knowing it she'd probably been waiting for years for him to carve his own personal entrance in the lounge wall with a chainsaw — looks as if the rain's easing off a bit. Let's go have a look at that sign, shall we?

"There she is," said Sam, leaning the sign against a sagging fence. "Pahau Valley Hotel. Doug Welsh, proprietor, Licensed to sell spirituous and fermented liquors. Let's have another go at the front door, Jack. They should be stirring by now." They hammered on the door, shook it, kicked it and called out.

"It's no use," said Jack disgustedly. "Whoever's in there just doesn't want visitors."

"Let's have a look round the back," said Sam. "There might be a duck or something we can knock off."

"There's drums of something in this old shed," called Jack, peering through a chink in the door. "But it's locked up."

"Here's the washhouse," said Sam. "It stinks like a brewery. Looks like they keep all the stale beer in the tubs." He tilted the window open as far as it would go and pushed his arm through the opening.

"Cider! Apple cider!" he exclaimed, licking his fingers. "Liquors eh? We'll half-inch a few pints of this if we can get it out. Not the best idea of a square meal, but it'll keep us warm."

They found a twelve-gallon cream can behind the shed and rinsed it out under a tap at the side of the building. A fruit jar was cleaned for a dipper, but was too big to go through the gap between the sill and the bottom of the window.

"Here, Jack, I'll give you a leg up. See if you can reach down and pull the plug."

With slightly less trouble than the cider was worth, Jack managed to hook the plug out with a piece of wire.

"Let 'er run for a bit to clean the drain out," said Sam. "Then we'll catch it in our jar and tip it into the can."

From the drain under the washhouse window they caught enough cider to nearly fill their can. They had to take it all because they couldn't get the plug back in.

"There's about ten gallons here," said Sam, as they carried the can between them to the truck. "That'll make up for their lack of hospitality. We'll just have to see how far we can get on what petrol we've got left now."

They filled their jar, put the can on the back, and drove off down the road.

"Not a bad drop," said Sam, sampling the cider. "Here, have a snort, Jack."

Half a mile on they stuttered round a bend and saw a big white building back off the road with two cars parked outside and a big sign saying "Pahau Valley Hotel. Doug Welsh, proprietor, licensed to sell spirituous and fermented liquors."

"Well, I'll go to hell," said Sam, lowering the cider jar.

"Food," cried Jack, "and a petrol pump!"

They pushed the Ford the last thirty yards to the bowser and went into the bar.

"Morning, boys," said an elderly barman who was wiping glasses behind the bar. "What'll you have?"

"A feed if you've got it," said Sam.

"I'll see if you're in time for breakfast." He went to a door and yelled, "Can you manage breakfast for two hungry men?"

"Send them round," called a woman's voice, after a few moments.

"Go through here and down the passage to the end," said the barman, holding open the door. "Missus Welsh'll fix you up."

"Thanks," said Jack. "You've saved us from a terrible death."

"Yeah, I know what it's like. Saved myself half an hour ago."

Mrs Welsh was a tired grey woman who was evidently used to rough men coming in late for breakfast. Jack's fears that there wouldn't be enough were groundless. They thanked her and returned to the bar, where already a group of sheepy looking men were drinking five-ounce beers.

"You chaps come far this morning?" asked the barman, pouring two beers.

"Camped by the old place back up the road here," said Sam. "What do we owe you for the feed?"

"Five bob each. That old shack used to be the pub, you know. Built this place and shifted in about four years ago now. The roadman's been living in the old place since then. He died about six weeks ago. Used to make his own home-brew. Drank himself to death with it if you ask me. His old lady's still there. Crazier than he was. Thinks people are trying to break in all the time. They'll come and get her one of these days. She must be starving to death by this time. There's no food gone into the place since her old man died. God knows what she's living on. When her old man was on the go they both used to make home-brew. They argued for years whose brew was the best. Drunk every day from sampling the stuff and fighting and abusing each other something terrible. In the finish they each sent a sample off to the Department of Scientific and Industrial Research to be tested. An urgent telegram came back for them saying: SHOOT BOTH HORSES. So they were no better off than ever and went on arguing and bickering right up until the night the old boy died."

Sam and Jack managed a weak laugh, then lapsed into thoughtful silence. Jack concentrated on his glass of beer and Sam finally said, "Tough on the old girl. Still, you never know but what we might end up like that."

"Yes," said the barman soberly. "You never know, do you?" "Can we get a few gallons of petrol off you?" asked Jack, to break another silence.

"Sure, how much do you want?"

"As much as we can get in the tank and the tin on the back."

"Right. Here's the key, you can pump it out yourselves."

With all the stones in the tank you could only get two and a half gallons in.

"What do you think about the old roadman's missus, Sam?" asked Jack, turning the pump handle to fill the four-gallon tin.

"Makes a man feel a bit lousy, doesn't it. Would you like a cider?"

"Hell, no! Couldn't face the blasted stuff after that."

"We'll tip it out as soon as we get out of sight of the pub. I can understand how a man could drink himself to death on it. We could probably run the jalopy on it if we got stuck for gas again."

"Might even finish the truck off or get us into trouble for driving a drunken vehicle," said Jack.

UNCLE WALLY

A mile beyond the Pahau pub Sam stopped the truck and they both got out. "One of these was the cause of us having to shift to another district when I was a young feller," said Sam, tipping the cream can so that the cider splashed and frothed all over the road.

"What, home-brew?"

"No, a cream can."

"An ordinary cream can?"

"The dead spitting image of this one," answered Sam, pushing the empty can upright and getting back into the truck. They drove on towards a rolling stretch of open sheep country that hung in the air away down the valley. Sam reached for the tobacco.

"What happened about this cream can, Sam?"

"Well, I s'pose I must have been about eight or ten at the time, living with my Uncle Wally who brought me up because my parents were poor and bred like rabbits. My uncle took me for the school holidays when brother Dick was born and hung on to me because I was good with the cows. There were so many kids at home I don't think they even noticed one was missing. Anyway they never asked for me back so I just stayed where I was. Uncle Wally had three hundred acres that he'd brought into grass all by himself and every time we'd go along the flats to fix a gate or something he'd say, 'Y'know, Sammy, this was all swamp when I came here. Rushes and scrub this high.' And he'd hold his hand way up over my head to show me how high it was. 'Look at it now,' he'd say, stopping and looking all around. 'One of the best little paddocks on the farm.' Or when we were spreading manure by hand on the hills he'd sit on a bag of super and say, 'Y'know, Sammy, this was all manuka and fern when I came here. Right where we're sitting there was a mass of tea-tree this thick.' He'd hold his hands spread apart to show me how thick. 'Now it's one of the best paddocks on the farm,' he'd say. I used to hate working on the boundary fence because it had been all bush up there and

89

the logs used to get bigger every time he told me about them. He'd chopped them all down with an axe. That was one of the best paddocks on the farm too."

"But how about this cream can?" said Jack, slowing down to pass a long mob of sheep and a cigarette-rolling, spur-wearing, hat-tilted, dog-cursing, horse-leading drover.

"Oh yes, the cream can. Well, every morning I used to bring the cows in while Uncle Wally boiled a billy of tea to bring over to the shed. After milking I'd have breakfast and run down to the road to catch the school bus. At night I'd get home in time to help finish the milking and cleaning up.

"Every morning, while Uncle Wally was away feeding the pigs, I used to run my fingers through the cream and lick them, until one morning he came into the separator room and caught me at it. After that he'd look for finger marks in the froth on the cream. It was about a week before I got the idea of tilting the can till the cream came to the lip. Then I could have a sly slurp and carefully sit the can back without leaving any marks on the froth. Got pretty good at it too, with a bit of practice.

"Then winter came and the cows started drying off. There got to be only one can of cream and then only half a can. There was only about four gallons the morning I had my head inside the can slurping happily away when I heard Uncle Wally's gumboots coming down the yard. I had a last lick and went to pull my head out, but my ears got caught and I couldn't for the life of me get my head out of the can. If I live to be a hundred, Jack," said Sam, gravely shaking his head at the memory, "I'll never collect another kick in the backside like the one Uncle Wally gave me when he came in and saw me with my head in the cream can.

" 'Get out of there,' he said.

" 'Can't, I'm stuck,' says I. And he grabbed me by the collar and just about tore the ears fair off me. Aunt Sarah came down with soapy water but nothing would shift me out of that can or the can off me. They rang the doctor and he said the only thing to do was to take me to the factory to have the can cut off. He said he'd be there to help when they got me there. Uncle Wally lifted the can, with me hanging out the top, on to the old konaki, and took me down to the creamstand. I was feeling pretty uncomfortable by the time the cream lorry came, I can tell you. The driver laughed fit to bust and said that happened to a cat he had with a jam jar, and they broke the jar. They just about broke my neck getting me up on to the truck, and my heart getting me to the factory.

"There I was, standing on the back of the truck, blind and gasping with splashing cream. Every time we stopped to pick up somebody's cream, they'd laugh their heads off and say how they'd go about getting me out. One of them said I was just a glutton and wouldn't pull my head out till I'd finished all the cream. Every now and again there'd be a great hooting and jeering to let me know we were passing groups of kids waiting for the school bus.

"At the factory they put me and my can on a trolley and wheeled me from one department to the other showing me to everyone. I was howling and just about drowned by the time they started working on the can with a gas torch. If they'd known what I was thinking of doing when I got out they'd have left me there. The heat from the cutting-torch set up such a smoking and fuming of burnt cream inside the can that I just about choked and Uncle Wally, who'd ridden in the front of the truck, and the doctor, who'd just arrived, made them stop. They sent away for a drill and bored a hole in the bottom of the can to drain the cream out.

"Then someone said, 'What's this?' and someone else said, 'It looks like lead.'

"Uncle Wally said, 'How did that get there?' and someone said, 'You ought to know, mate. We'll have to get the manager to have a look at this.'

"The manager came and after a lot of questions and answers he said he wanted to see Uncle Wally in his office. He sent the truck back to the farm for the rest of Uncle Wally's cream cans — and me with my head still stuck in the can. The doctor and two other blokes shoved a sack down the back of my neck and they cooked me out. They had to cut the can to bits and the heat just about done me in. The bloke with the cutting-torch told the doctor what about leaving the top of the can on me for a collar so I'd be easy to catch but the doctor said for him to watch what he was doing

91

or he'd catch me on fire. The moment I straightened up I went out like a light. I woke up in my bed at home and the doctor was telling Aunt Sarah how I'd had a shock and had to rest and be looked after. I don't know about the shock, but I certainly got a fright when I remembered about the lead in the bottom of the cream can."

"How's that Sam?" asked Jack. "Is lead bad for the cream?"

"No, it wasn't that. You see, they used to put the cans on the scales, deduct the weight of an empty twelve-gallon can and pay you for the weight of cream. Uncle Wally had a half-inch layer of lead in the bottom of his cans. Must have done the factory for quite a few bob before they found it. I was a little worried in case he blamed me, but he didn't say a word about it.

"By the time I was fit to get around again, people were coming to look at the farm. Uncle Wally would take them down the flats and say, 'Y'know, this was all swamp when I came here. Rushes and scrub this high.' Up the back he'd tell them about the 'tea-tree this thick' and the 'logs that big'.

"When the farm was sold we shifted on to a small sheep-run at Paparimu and Uncle Wally bought three dogs and a pup. When the pup was two years old he used to take visitors down to the kennels and say, 'Y'know, that dog was just a pup when I got him. Little feller was only about this big.' And he'd hold his hands close together to show them how big. 'Now he's one of the best dogs in the district,' he'd say.

"Ah, here's a bit of open country at last. All sheep and cattle round here by the looks of it."

"Are we looking for another job yet, Sam?" asked Jack, still grinning about Uncle Wally.

"There's no desperate hurry. We've got a few bob in the kick and enough squirt in the old bus to get us around the country till we find somewhere that needs two experienced blokes. A little holiday isn't going to do us any harm. You grow old quick if you work too hard anyway. We'll find something to do before we go broke."

"Good idea," agreed Jack. "What's the country like up Gisborne way?"

"Not bad. All the farms are sliding into the sea and the roads are no better than this, but there's a nice little patch of bush round the Waioeka Gorge. Deer, pigs, possums, goats and jobs to make a living out of. Shall we go up and have a look at it?"

"Wouldn't mind," said Jack. "Haven't been to Gisborne yet. What's the town like, Sam?"

"Pub on every corner and crawling with rich cockies in flash cars. Tons of dough round the place."

"This track should take us out to the main coast road pretty soon. Probably be having a beer in the old Masonic by this time tomorrow."

Three and a half hours later they came to an automatic stop at a building that sprawled out behind a sign proclaiming it to be the Morere Hotel.

"Might as well sink one or two while we're here," said Sam. "It'll break up the trip and give the bomb a chance to rest 'er feet."

"I could use a beer meself," said Jack, leading the way towards the public bar door.

The barman had the place to himself. "Two big ones, thanks mate," said Sam. "What's the beer?"

"Cascade. A nice drop too. Nothing but the best here."

"How far to Gisborne?" asked Jack.

"Thirty-six mile. Takes just under an hour from here."

A leathery, whiskery, hobnail-booted man growled at dogs from the door and came into the bar.

"Beer?" asked the barman.

The man nodded and put a pound note on the bar.

"Whose beardie on the truck out there?" he said.

"Ours," said Sam.

"Want to sell him?"

"No."

"How much do you want for him?"

"We've been told to name our own price many a time."

"I'll give you a fiver for him."

"Now just hang on a minute there, mate," said Sam, moving along the bar towards the newcomer. You know Harvey Wilson, the dog breeder?"

"Can't say I do."

"Well you can't buy one of Harvey's dogs for a fiver. His

93

beardies have been taking all the big prizes in the overseas dog trials. His pups are sold before they're born and there's a waiting list from here to the other end of the bar long. Harvey himself gave us that dog when we rescued his best breeding bitch from a rock in the middle of a flooded river. A man'd be almost betraying a trust to sell Royal Harvill Span there — and you offer us a fiver!"

"A tenner," said the dog-man. "And that's as high as I'll go." He turned to his drink as though he wasn't really interested in the dog anyway.

"Well, that's that," said Sam, emptying his glass. "We couldn't let him go for a penny under fifteen quid."

They had another drink, said thank you to the barman and went out to the truck.

"Hang on," called the dog-man, coming out after them. "Do you reckon that dog's worth fifteen quid?"

"No," said Sam, turning, "he's worth more than twice that. We've got to get rid of him because we haven't got any work for him. He's too good a dog to make a pet out of."

"Okay. Fifteen quid." And he peeled three fivers off the biggest roll of money that Jack had ever seen.

"You don't want a good rifle by any chance?" asked Sam, eyeing the handful of notes.

"No, just the dog'll do me." And he took the cowman gardener's beardie, tying him among four other dogs in the back of his Land Rover.

"We'll post old Ben a fiver of this when we get to a post office," said Sam. "Have to tell him the dog got run over and the bloke who did it gave us five quid compo."

"That's a tenner profit for us," said Jack. "Do you think the dog was worth that much?"

"The dog was worth about thirty bob," replied Sam. "But that bloke had more than his share of money anyway, and that's the dog off our hands. Won't have to worry about feeding him now."

HARD GRAFTING

Sam and Jack carried a wet sack of mussels into the porch of their new home, a leaning hut that stood at the end of the road. It looked out over a wide river that spread, a hundred yards on, into a scythe-blade east coast bay. Inside were a row of well-stocked food shelves, two uncomfortable bunks, and a driftwood fire. Sam stirred the fire and threw more wood into the blaze while Jack went to the river to fill their water tin. Mussels and bread were cooked and eaten. The tea billy and two pairs of socks steamed comfortably by the fire.

"What do you think of Tom Sanders, Sam?" asked Jack, reaching for the mugs.

"He'll be all right to work for," said Sam. "As long as he leaves us alone to do the job our way and in our time it couldn't be better."

"Nice little hut this. Do you think many people come here?"

"Oh, I s'pose we'll get the odd bloke or two come out for a bit of fishing or rabbiting, but I don't think we're likely to get flooded with visitors."

"Do you think Tom believed about us doing a forty-mile fencing contract for Harvey Wilson?"

"Course he did. That's why he was so anxious to get us out here. There's nothing in it anyhow. We'll have all the posts and battens and strainers split in a month or two and the fence finished in another three months."

"He wants us to pull down that old fence between the road paddock and the river before we start on the big job, to make a winter run for the hoggets," said Jack, who'd just returned from a visit to the homestead.

"That won't take two experienced men long," said Sam.

"He's paying us a full day so if we get it done early, we can take the rest of the day off."

"Good. We'll get a bit of fishing in," said Sam. "I've got a couple of new rigs to try out."

"If we start early we might even get it done by lunch time," suggested Jack.

"Depends whether he wants us to save the good posts and wire, Jack."

"No, he said to throw it all in the river."

"In that case all we have to do is dig the posts out and roll them up in a big bundle, battens, wire and all, and tip 'er in and — y'know, Jack, I once caused a bloke's death by pulling down a few chain of old fence."

"Hell, Sam! Did a bull get out?"

"No, there was nothing in the paddock."

"Well, how did it happen?"

"It was about twelve years ago now, but I can remember as though it was yesterday. Shook me up a bit, I can tell you.

"Another bloke and I had been working in the bush in behind Motu and we went into Gisborne to cash our cheques and play merry hell for a couple of weeks. The first day in town we got into a lift to go up and see his brother who worked in an office. My mate slammed the outside door of the lift on the end of his overcoat, and pushed the button — smack! He got dragged up against the inside door so hard his shoulder got pulled out of joint.

"While I was waiting for him to come out of hospital I met a cocky in the pub, who offered me a job for two days, stripping an old fence. Took me up to his place, in behind Waioeka, and stuck me in a hut with the dirtiest old coot I've ever come across. I tell you, Jack me boy, that bloke was so dirty I had to sleep under the tankstand. Couldn't bear the stink. He told me he was going over the hill to a 'do' with some scrub-cutters the next day.

"The fence I had to pull down ran straight up the hill from this bloke's hut and joined one that ran along the top of a ridge. It was in a hell of a mess! Took me all next day to get it stripped.

"The old bloke never came back that night and when the boss came down with some meat for us next day he decided to ride over to the scrub-cutters' hut to see if everything was all right. He came back two hours later and said the old boy had left his mates, tight as a winch-rope, at about ten o'clock the night before.

" 'Why didn't they give him a bunk for the night if he was s̱ shikker?' I asked him. And he said:

" 'Oh, old Fred always walks back from over there absolutely rotten. I've seen him make it on a pitch black night when it was raining so hard you could hardly stand up in it. He just follows the fence line.'

"Then I woke up!

" 'If he carried on along the ridge past here, where would he end up?' I asked.

" 'Fair in the river,' he said. 'But old Fred's been doing that trip for so long he must know every post by now.'

" 'Not if he used this old fence to mark his turnoff,' I said. 'I pulled 'er down yesterday.'

"And sure enough, they dredged old Fred out of the river next day. He'd walked fair over a bluff into a gorge at the end of the fence."

Sam picked up his mug, then put it down again.

"About a month after that I was working with a bloke who'd put up a fence while his boss was away on holiday. The boss came back and rode a horse into it at full gallop in the dark next morning. Tore his leg to bits on the barbed wire.

"She's a dangerous caper all right. Never know what you're going to come up against in this fencing business. A mate and I were battening up on the last stretch of a road fence one night and some galoot ups and drives his car fair through the strainer. Took us two days to clean up the mess. And then they had to cut the wires in a different place to drag what was left of the car out."

"Did the driver get hurt?" asked Jack.

"No. My mate couldn't catch him . . . And then there was the time Uncle Wally noticed that the new boundary fence our neighbour had slugged him half the costs of was about six feet on Uncle Wally's side of the survey pegs. They had a hell of a stink over it and in the end Uncle Wally and I went up to shift it back to the right line. Uncle Wally grabbed one of the wires and collected about four thousand volts in one hit. The neighbour had her hooked on to a transformer at the other end. Must have taken him about half a day to rig it up, but it changed Uncle Wally's mind about shifting the fence. He decided to take the neighbour to court, but he never ever got round to doing it. As far as I know the fence is still six feet over Uncle Wally's boundary."

It took them all next day to pull the old fence down so they took the following day off to make up for it. The fish weren't biting as well as their reputation promised.

"We'll get stuck into the job tomorrow, Jack me boy," said Sam, blowing out their candle that night. "First one to wake up swings the billy."

They were up at daylight and felled a big totara in a patch of bush up the river and split it into posts and battens. Next day they did another and the day after that another; until they had eight thousand battens, two thousand posts and fifty strainers piled in stacks in the bush above the hut. Jack's blisters were vanishing and he could hit the flitches in exactly the right place to split out a post or batten like Sam did. The day they finished stacking the last pile of battens was wet, so they went back to the hut early and Sam worked out that they'd earned six hundred and thirty-five pounds in the nine weeks it had taken them. To Jack, this was an unbelievable amount of money for an unbelievable amount of work, and they still had to clear the fence line, lay out the material and erect nearly four miles of boundary fence along the coast. They'd be rolling in dough when the job was cut.

"Now that we've got all the stuff ready we can sit back and enjoy ourselves for a while," said Sam. "Where's our fishing lines, Jack? We might as well get them ready to use in case it's fine tomorrow. I'll fix up a few cartridges for the old shotgun so we can have a bash at those pigs you saw the other day."

"I wish we had some pig-dogs," said Jack. "There's a lot of heavy scrub up there that we'd never be able to stalk them in."

"The evening's the caper," said Sam. "We'll get one or two when they come out into the clearings just before dark. We can fish and loaf during the day and hunt in the evenings. There's probably enough fish in the bay here to feed old mother Pringle's cats!"

"Whose cats?"

"Old lady Pringle. Lived in a big house next door to us on a farm Uncle Wally was sharemilking on when I was a kid," answered Sam, reaching for the tobacco. "It started off, the, reckoned, about two years before we came there. The old girl took a liking to a stray cat that was hanging round and started feeding it. Before she knew where she was she had a litter on her hands. By the time we arrived there were about two hundred of them."

"Two hundred, Sam? Cut it out!"

"Fair go, Jack. Uncle Wally had a go at counting them once or twice but he lost count when he got up around the hundred and thirty mark because they used to move about too much. We sold the old lady six gallons of milk every day to feed them on, and she got about half a ton of cat's-meat delivered every week. You'd see her coming down the calf paddock in the morning with her two buckets and hundreds of cats streaming after her, miaowing and screeching like they'd never had a feed in their lives. They'd be coming from under sheds and hay stacks and out of the scrub and the hay paddock and the fern along the edge of the road and under the house and the hedges, and all over the farm. You'd wonder when the hell it was going to stop. Aunt Sarah used to say it looked like the Pied Piper of Hamilton. While mother Pringle was getting her milk the cats would swarm round the shed like mothers around the post office on family benefit day and then follow her back to the house to get fed.

"Stink! Jack me boy, you just wouldn't believe it! The old girl got to letting the cats into the house on wet nights. Her old man packed his bluey in the finish. He couldn't sit down anywhere but what a cat was having kittens there. He tried to get a divorce on the grounds that his wife kept cats in the house but they turned the poor coot down. Uncle Wally said it was because the judge wouldn't believe there was that many cats in the country, let alone at Darcy Pringle's place, and he thought old Darcy was pulling his leg. Anyhow he never came back to the district till all the cats were gone."

"Did she sell them to get her husband back?" asked Jack.

"No, after a while a terrible disease got into them. Cats dying all over the place, screechin' their rotten heads off! Uncle Wally and I had to keep running outside to chase the cats that came to die under our house. Big sticks we had, thrashing and shooting like herding sheep into the dip. Uncle Wally bought a fox terrier, but it got beaten up by a gang of toms and spent all its time hiding from them after that."

"What did she do with the dead cats?" asked Jack.

"She laid them out in the washhouse and the shed where Darcy used to keep his car. You see, the old lady was a bit crackers on it and she thought they were only sick — stiff as boards and stinkin' they were by this time."

"I bet it'd smell, Sam."

"Smell? Jack me boy," said Sam imploringly, "have you ever smelt a dead horse or shot an old billy-goat on a hot day? Have you ever caught a stoat in a rabbit trap? Jack, if I live to be a thousand I'll never forget the way old lady Pringle's place stank with those dead cats. I just can't describe it." Sam spread his hands helplessly.

"Did she ever get round to burying them?" asked Jack, hoping the yarn wasn't finished yet.

"Well, everyone was talking about ringing the police because whenever the wind blew towards them from her place they had to go out for the day. And our house was dead in line with the prevailing wind. We went to town every day for a week, the cows were holding their milk and you couldn't catch the horses to save yourself. In the end the old lady called the cops herself. Reckoned someone was poisoning her cats. They took one look and went straight back to town. Next day the County Council blokes came and dug big holes to bury the cats in. Then they sprayed the house and sheds with disinfectant. Took them four days, and even after they'd gone we still found a dead cat whenever we moved a bale of hay or lifted a board or post or a piece of tin.

"After that mother Pringle went into a home or something and when Darcy came back, about a month later, a few stray survivors were starting to come round again. Poor old Darcy, I think it got on his mind a bit. He used to patrol his boundary with a shotgun, muttering like a public bar and shooting wildly at every cat he came across. Every time Uncle Wally or I met him he'd say: 'Any cats? Seen any cats?' and look around to see if we were sneaking one on to his place. It wasn't safe to go too near Darcy's place after dark because the slightest bit of noise had him rushing out with his shotgun, blazing away towards where he thought he'd heard a cat."

"He must have been in a pretty bad way all right," said Jack. "Did he end up in the nut-house too?"

"Don't know what happened to old Darcy in the finish. He was still going strong when Uncle Wally's horse won the big race at Epsom and we had to leave the district."

"A racehorse?"

"Yep! A fair dinkum thoroughbred mongrel of a pacer called Tallfern. Dirtiest-tempered, ugliest ratbag of a horse you ever saw in your life. More white in his eye than a Maori with a green eel on his hook. Uncle Wally bought him off a Chinaman for two cows and thirty quid, and poured more oats, chaff, hay, good grass, time and bot-bombs into his miserable hide than all the cows were getting between them. We made a track to train him on and every morning I had to get the milking started while Tallfern got his workout. Uncle Wally used to say how he was going to play merry hell with his horse at the races and Aunt Sarah said the only playing he'd ever do was 'Remembrance' on its ribs with a guitar pick.

"When the trotting season started at Epsom, Uncle Wally bought a brand-new sulky and patched up all the harness. Then he had to have a trailer and horseshoes and entry fees and more bot-bombs. Aunt Sarah and I listened on the wireless to the first race Tallfern was in but he was only mentioned once. Somewhere near the start of the race the announcer said: 'And six lengths further back to Tallfern!' I think they had to wait for him to get off the track so they could start the next race. The bit had come out of his mouth and Uncle Wally couldn't pull him up when the race ended.

"When he came home Uncle Wally said how he'd had a bit of bad luck, but he couldn't possibly lose the big race the next Saturday. Aunt Sarah said he'd better not or we'd lose our account at the store.

"We lost our account at the store. It got so we'd have boiled mangels and mutton for tea every night so there could be oats and bot-bombs and entry fees and things. Uncle Wally still swore he'd just been unlucky last week and he couldn't lose next Saturday, but Aunt Sarah and I didn't even listen on the radio any more.

"Then came the great day. Tallfern won a race by half the length of the straight. The first we heard of it was when Uncle Wally came home early — in an ambulance."

"An ambulance?" cried Jack.

"Yeah. Bruised and burnt all over. He was in bed for two weeks."

Sam spat into the fire.

"What happened?" asked Jack.

"Well Uncle Wally used to feel the cold a fair bit so he wore his old leather coat under his racing mocker. When the race was due to start he knocked out his pipe on the sulky shaft and stuffed it in the pocket of his jacket. It wasn't out properly and when they started racing the wind fanned the sparks until Uncle Wally's coat suddenly burst into flames. He was in amongst a bunch of other horses at the time and they shied off in all directions. That put most of them out of the race. By the time they came into the straight there were horses and drivers and broken sulkies scattered all round the track. Tallfern suddenly saw what was going on and he galloped past the post like Johnny Globe. Uncle Wally was blazing like a forge and let go one of the reins to try and beat the fire out — and they shot through the rails into the crowd. Four people got knocked around and the horse broke its leg. Had to be destroyed. They put Uncle Wally out and brought him home all done up in bandages and instructions.

"The racing club suspended him for a year for being careless, and Aunt Sarah and I had to do the milking till he recovered. It was worth it though, because we knew there'd be no more racehorses and bot-bombs.

"All the kids got to know about it and teased me so I didn't want to go to school. Uncle Wally said not to be a sissy and made me go. Then all the neighbours started pointing and snickering and staring at him when he went past, so he made up hundreds of excuses why we should move to another place. We shifted on to a poultry farm at Henderson and started breeding pigs."

"Bit of a come-down from racehorses to pigs," observed Jack, with a grin.

"No fear," said Sam, "we ate on the pig farm. Bacon and eggs for breakfast, dinner and tea. No matter how much Uncle Wally spent on his money-making ideas, you were never short of a feed. Ate ourselves out of business in the finish — cleaned up the pigs, got sick of eggs and chooks, and sold out to an English couple who wanted a 'small holding' — left them holding the bag if you ask me."

Sam and Jack gave themselves a month off on the strength of the perfect weather. They sat in the sun and read the few books that someone had left in the hut. They dug cockles out of the sand and gathered mussels among the rocks at low tide and feasted on the beach.

They stood on the rocks at the end of the bay and swung their lines into the surf to catch the snapper, kahawai, cod and tarakihi that Tom Sanders had told them boiled in the surf in shoals the size of quarter-acre sections. The few vague nibbles that rewarded their hours of bait-changing, place-shifting patience might have been bites — or might not have. But they sneaked along the scrub-edge in the evenings and bowled wild pigs with their shotgun.

They made a raft out of two logs and poled it up the river, exploring from bend to bend, and then drifted lazily back to the hut on the slow current. They found a wild beehive and Sam showed Jack how to get the honey.

When their supply of food ran out they spent a day doing odd repairs to their truck, then made a trip to town. On their way they called in to see Tom Sanders at the homestead and told him they were ready to start on the fence line. He gave them a progress payment and said he'd send out a couple of men on a tractor to lay the posts and wire along the fence line for them.

It took them eight days to clear the line and help lay the materials along it. Then for three weeks they dug post- and strainer-holes, ran out wires, footed posts, blocked and stayed the angles, strained up, tied off, tacked up and hung battens.

"We've just about worn ourselves a road along here," said Sam, as he and Jack walked back along the completed fence to the hut for the last time.

"Yeah," grinned Jack. "You'd think a mob of cattle had been chased through the joint."

"Forty chain in three weeks in this sort of country is pretty good going," said Sam. "How does it feel to be an experienced fencer, Jack?"

"Sick of the sight of post-holes and wire," replied Jack, laughing.

"At a fiver a chain, that's two hundred quid to play round with, and we've still got five hundred to collect for the posts and battens we split."

"I see what you mean," said Jack. "Better than twelve pound ten a week in a factory making coat-hangers or pencil cases.'

"Not counting the month we had off, we average about twenty-five quid a week each for the time we've been here," worked out Sam. "We could buy ourselves a nice little truck to run around in if you feel like it."

"I'll say," said Jack enthusiastically. "No more stones and hoses and draughts and leaks! What'll we get, Sam?"

"I think we'd better have a look around when we get to town," replied Sam. "Might even pay us to go through to Napier and see what they've got there. A man can run himself into no end of trouble by buying the first thing he claps his eyes on."

"I suppose you're right," said Jack, leading the way into the hut. "I'll be glad to get rid of old Gertie. How much do you think we'll get for her?"

" 'Bout a fiver for a trade-in," said Sam. "Tenner if we're lucky."

"But she cost me thirty quid," cried Jack.

"Well, we've had more than thirty quid's worth of running out of the old girl," pointed out Sam, "so you make a fair profit."

Jack had to agree.

They stood, with their booted feet on the low fence and seven hundred pounds in Jack's hip pocket, looking at two long rows of gleaming used cars and trucks. "Drover Road Car Dealers Ltd," read the sign.

"We've had a pretty good run out of the old Ford," said Sam. "What say we get a later model?"

"Suits me," said Jack. "Nice lookin' green job along there. Just our size. Two-fifty deposit, it says on the windscreen."

"Let's have a look at it, shall we?" suggested Sam.

No sooner had they entered the yard than a hair-oily man with the cleanest white shirt Jack had ever seen came hurrying out of a caravan to meet them, grinning like a court-case.

"Good morning," he slopped. "Can I show you gentlemen something?"

"Just havin' a squiz at the Ford here," said Sam.

"Well, now. It's funny you should have picked this one because, between you and me, it's the best thing at seven sixty-five I've had in for a long time.

"We haven't picked it yet," pointed out Sam in what Jack knew was his "I don't like the look of this bloke" voice.

"Perhaps you gentlemen would like to go for a ride in it," said the dealer. "I'll just put another battery in it for you. This one's a bit flat to turn her over."

He changed the battery while Sam and Jack had a look over the rest of the truck. Then they drove it round the block. The dealer was waiting to pounce when they got back to the yard.

"How do you like her?" he asked.

"Fair enough," said Sam.

"Yes, I knew you'd fall in love with her. There's several people after that one."

"Why haven't they bought it?" asked Sam.

"When would you want to take delivery?" asked the dealer, ignoring Sam's question.

"Today," said Sam.

"Ah. Good. If you'll just come across to the office I'll fill out your hire purchase agreement."

"We'll pay cash," said Sam.

The dealer sidled over towards the caravan bowing like a manuka-bush in a strong wind.

"I'll make out a receipt for the seven sixty-five pounds ten for you," he said.

"Six seventy-five," said Sam.

The dealer stopped in mid-stride. "But that one's seven sixty-five."

"We'll give you six seventy-five for it," said Sam.

"I'm sorry, sir, but I couldn't possibly come down that much. For cash I might be able to let you have it for seven fifty."

Sam suddenly came to life —

"Now just hang on a minute there, mate!" he said, leaning back against a handy mudguard. "That sort of thing might go down with most blokes, but it's got no show with anyone who's flogged cars for Harvey Wilson for six years."

The car dealer was clearly exasperated.

"I don't care who the hell you flogged cars for and how long you flogged them. I tell you I can't let this vehicle go for a penny under seven fifty. I paid more than that for it."

"Six seventy-five," quoted Sam.

"Now look here," cried the dealer. "What sort of fool do you take me for?"

"Well, it was you who wanted us to pay seven sixty-five for a forty-six model," said Sam. "More hide than an old boar, some of you blokes."

"Seven twenty-five," said the dealer with finality. "You can take it or leave it."

Sam and Jack drove away in their new truck. Their old one they had left in a wrecker's yard, lonely as a flat tyre.

"Hard man, Jack," said Sam gravely. "But even at six seventy-five quid I'll bet he still makes a few bob out of it."

"I don't know," said Jack doubtfully. "Looked to me as though he was more interested in getting rid of us than making money, in the finish there."

"Ah well, that's not to worry, Jack me boy. Listen to that motor. Like rain on the roof after the old tractor we just got rid of. I reckon we were lucky enough to get twenty notes for the old girl, at that."

"I'll say," said Jack, grinning at the memory of their half hour in the wrecker's yard. "I thought that bloke was going to start howling on us. You were a bit tough on him, Sam."

"Don't worry about those coots, Jack me boy. They'll take you down as quick as look at you. Biggest heap of thieves a man's ever likely to run into!"

NOT GUILTY, SIR

"Samuel Cash," intoned the clerk of the court, squatting in his enclosure below the magistrate.

"Samuel Cash," echoed the court orderly, and the cop in the corner held open the door as Sam strode through.

After glancing at his papers, the clerk looked across at Sam, who was now standing in the dock.

"Samuel Cash, you are charged that on the seventeenth of September last you were idle and disorderly, being found on the premises of the Wanganui Unitarian Church without lawful excuse. How do you plead?"

"Ah — not guilty, sir," said Sam.

The clerk went through the same procedure with Jack. The charge was read out and he was asked how he pleaded.

"Not guilty," said Jack with a doubtful look at Sam beside him in the dock.

The sergeant asked if the accused had any objection to their cases being heard together, and when Sam and Jack said they didn't mind, he called the constable who had nabbed them the night before. A young man, blushing furiously, entered the witness box, standing rigid while the orderly gave him the Bible for the oath.

"Sir, on the night of the seventeenth of September last, at eleven pm while on duty I discovered the accused and another on the premises of the Wanganui Unitarian Church," said the constable in parrot fashion. "Neither of them could offer any excuse for being there beyond that they were looking for somewhere to sleep. I then arrested them and escorted them to the police station. There was one pound, eleven shillings and tenpence on the accused when charged."

The magistrate's glasses glinted like pools of water in the dim Friday courtroom. He peered at Sam, who leaned on the rail of the dock, looking round.

"I understand you are conducting your own defence," he said. "Do you wish to ask the witness any questions?"

"No, I don't think so," said Sam. "It'd be a waste of time."

"Do you wish to ask the witness any questions?" the magistrate asked Jack in turn.

Jack shook his head. He was scared stiff.

The sergeant said that was the police case against the accused and sat down.

The magistrate explained that Sam and Jack could call witnesses if they had any available, or they could give evidence in the witness box on their own behalf. If they did this however they would be liable to cross-examination. If they didn't want to go into the witness box and be cross-examined they could make statements from the dock.

"She's right," said Sam. "I'll just tell you our side of the story if you don't mind, sir. Will it be all right if I do the talking for me mate? He's only a young bloke and . . ."

"Yes, yes, that will be all right."

"Well, sir, me and Jack here were working on jobs round the Hawke's Bay, and then we decided to have a look what was going over this way. We finished off a fencing contract and bought a truck with most of the money. Then we lit off. We only had about thirty quid when we started but we done some draining for an old girl who's got a bit of a sheep-run on the Taihape Road and made fifteen quid.

"Then we built a stockyards for Bob Austin who runs the Awaroa station. Made forty quid out of that lot and nicked across to the Manawatu.

"Met a bloke in the Standard who reck —"

"And what is the Standard?" interrupted the magistrate.

"That's a pub. Burton's beer. It's the one with the deerhead over the door and the barman who . . ."

"That will do, we haven't yet heard how you come to be in Wanganui with no job or money."

"Coming to that, sir. Well, we ran into this bloke who offered us a job digging water-holes for sheep around the edge of a big swamp he had on his place. You should have seen 'er — half a mile round and all floating rushes and swamp-grass. You could

114

jump on a solid-looking bit and all the swamp shook for twenty or thirty yards. . . ."

"Jumping on swamps is not one of my recreations," said the magistrate. "Please get on with your story. The court is not interested in irrelevant details."

"Well, this bloke, Dan Porter, said he'd give us fifty quid to dig eighteen water-holes round the swamp to save the stock walking out into it and getting bogged down looking for water. He must have lost plenty of sheep too, because we found about thirty dead ewes. Stink! You never smelt . . ."

"The facts," said the magistrate wearily, tapping his bench with the ends of his fingers.

"Well, we dug the water-holes," continued Sam. "Made a pretty good job of it too. Took us nearly two weeks. We blew the last few holes with gelignite. You should have seen the mud fly!" he said enthusiastically. "One hunk — it must have been half a hundredweight — caught me mate here fair in the chest. Knocked him in a screaming heap."

"Please come to the point," said the magistrate. "We are not interested in the 'hunks of mud'."

"Sorry sir. I just wanted to tell you about how this hunk of mud skittled . . ."

"We don't *want* to hear how your friend was 'skittled' by some mud. You are wasting the court's time. Were you paid the fifty pounds for your digging?"

"Well yes and no, sir. You see, we collected our cheque and came to Wanganui for a look round. Spent nearly all our cash and then took the cheque into the bank. But she bounced on us. The bloke said to present it again or something. We reckoned we'd go back today and hammer the bloke who done it. Put us in the cart good and proper it did.

"We were sneaking to the church to bunk down last night when the johns lumbered us. Took all our stuff and locked us up like a pair of crooks or something." Sam glared accusingly at the sergeant with the shiny pants. Jack saw that the magistrate was trying not to smile.

"Why didn't you obtain legal advice about your dishonoured cheque?"

"Didn't think of it," said Sam, surprised.

"Hmmm. You have no job to go to and no money?"

"Oh, we'll soon get a job, sir. Me and Jack here can do anything. If it wasn't for Dan Porter and his rubber cheque we'd have been miles away by now. If we ever run into him again . . ."

"I hope you'll do the correct thing and discuss the matter with the proper authorities," said the magistrate, frowning sternly. "Taking the law into your own hands will not be tolerated by any court in this country. Do you understand?"

"Yes, sir. Only it was a lot of hard work to do for nothing."

The magistrate said there were official channels for dealing with allegations of false pretences. Then he asked the sergeant a series of questions about where the two men claimed to have been working and what was known about the £50 cheque.

"First the police have heard of any cheque, your worship," stated the sergeant. "Neither of the accused had any cheque in their possession when they were searched at the watch house."

"You didn't search us properly, that's why," said Sam triumphantly.

"Silence!" bawled the court orderly.

"Just a moment — where is this mysterious cheque now?" the magistrate wanted to know.

Sam bent down in the dock and fumbled at his feet. He reappeared flourishing a muddy shoe. From inside the toe he produced a dirty, folded slip of paper and passed it to the clerk.

"Exhibit A," intoned that dignitary, making an entry on the court file.

"Why did you hide it?" asked the magistrate after he had examined the cheque.

"I didn't want the bluebottles to get it," said Sam.

"That's enough," said the magistrate. "I'll accept your story, though I'm bound to point out that it's your own foolish and irregular behaviour which caused the police to act as they did. I think they were only doing their duty in arresting you. However I'm now satisfied from what you say that both of you have funds available to you and you both have work to go to. Under those circumstances I find that there is insufficient evidence for a conviction on charges of being idle and disorderly, and I think the proper course is to dismiss the information."

"Thank you, sir."

"You won't thank me if I find you before this court again. I strongly advise you to get yourselves into some kind of permanent employment."

"But we are, sir," said Sam. "We're permanently employed nicking here and there, doing odd little jobs for people who can't afford to pay a man all the year round. We never go short of work, sir. And it's only by accident that we got in the cactus this time."

"I see. Well, you'll have to make sure there are no more of these accidents. Information dismissed! Stand down."

Sam strode round to shake hands with the magistrate

"That's pretty decent of you, mate. Any time you . . ."

He was hurried away by the sergeant with the shiny pants and a constable who couldn't help grinning.

WOMEN!

"Nice bloke that judge, eh, Jack me boy, said Sam as they drove away from the police station after collecting all their gear. Jack still felt nervous.

"What are we going to do, Sam? We've hardly any petrol left and no way of getting any. And I'm getting hungry."

"Do you want some petrol?" asked Sam. "Why didn't you say so? Watch this!"

At the next service station Sam swung the Ford in by the pumps and stopped.

"Fill the old girl up, will you mate," he said to the attendant who came out of the office. "We've got a long way to go tonight. And you'd better check the oil, water and tyres for us too."

"Righto mate," said the attendant. "How many will she hold?"

"About fourteen and a pint of thirty ought to do her. She's a thirsty old bitch. Send us broke before she's finished."

The attendant laughed, and filled their tank.

Jack was horrified.

"Thirteen and a half," said the attendant, screwing the cap on their tank.

"Charge us for fourteen gallons and have a beer on us," said Sam expansively.

"Two pound six and a penny," said the attendant, closing the bonnet. Sam dug in his hip pocket.

"Hell's bloody teeth!" he cried disgustedly. "I've only got that fifty quidder on me. Got any notes, Bill?"

"No, I haven't," said Jack, watching the attendant's face.

"Don't s'pose you could manage to cash a fifty for us, mate?" asked Sam hopelessly.

"Not a show, mate. Banked this afternoon."

"That's just lovely, that is. And we've got to go right through to Hastings tonight."

"I could ring the boss. He might have the cash at home,"

said the attendant.

"Tell you what," said Sam, brightening. "Get the boss on the blower and let me talk to him."

The attendant took them into the office and dialled a number. Sam took the receiver.

"What's this bloke's name?" he asked.

"Scott. Charlie Scott."

"Hullo, hullo. Charlie Scott?" said Sam to the phone.

"Sam Cash here, Charlie. We're down at your garage. Bit of a balls-up down here. Got two quid's worth of gas off the bloke here and then found I only had a fifty quid cheque on me. — No, we tried that. Too late. — Well, I thought of leaving the cheque here with you but we probably won't be back this way for months. — Hastings. — Dan Porter. Know him? — Should be. He's got one of the biggest sheep-stations in the North Island. — Could you do that for us? — That's pretty decent of you, mate. I'll leave my address with the bloke here and you can post it on to me any time. — That's all right. We've got plenty of cash once we get to Hastings. — Okay. I'll put him on. Sorry to have caused the inconvenience. Won't forget it. — Right. Hooray.

"Boss wants to talk to you," said Sam, handing the receiver to the attendant, who listened for a few minutes, saying, "Yes — yes — okay," at intervals.

"That'll be all right mate," he said, hanging up. "Must have caught Charlie in a good mood. I'll just take your name and address. Got the cheque there?" Sam gave him the cheque and a careful address in Hastings.

They left.

"Are you sure we won't get into trouble over this?" asked Jack.

"Not a show," replied Sam cheerfully. "I gave them the address of some people who used to handle my mail when I was working up and down the coast. If the cheque bounces again we'll say we're terribly sorry and post them the cash."

Jack was very relieved at this and began to notice he was hungry again. They stopped at a store and bought a loaf of bread. Next stop was by a bridge, where they gathered a bundle of watercress. The third stop was up an old road that ran into a block of bush off the main road. Sam got out the shotgun.

122

"Light a fire and get our billy boiling, Jack me boy," he said. "I'll see if I can dig up a bit of meat." He went into the bush and half an hour later Jack heard three spaced shots. Sam returned with a plucked, bony pigeon and two rabbits.

"Got 'em on the other side of the bush. Should be fairly decent stew in them. Cut up the watercress into the billy while I skin the bunnies, Jack me boy. We'll eat tonight and think about a job tomorrow."

They ate their stew to the last burping scrape. Jack leaned back from the fire and wiped his greasy hands on the legs of his trousers.

"Might as well camp here for the night," said Sam, looking at the sky.

"It'll be about as comfortable as a hole in your pants," said Jack happily, stealing one of Sam's phrases.

"No fear," said Sam. "We've got our axe to cut wood for a fire and the cover for a roof in case it rains. We can take the seats out of the truck to sleep on."

"You're pretty good at working things out, Sam," Jack said admiringly.

"Getting cheeky now you've got a full guts, eh?" said Sam. "Who's going to cut the wood?"

They sat with their backs comfortably against a log. The fire glowed warmly on the trees around them. A possum skarkled in the dark bush and Jack was thinking how he wouldn't swap places with anyone in the world. Sam, puffing slowly on a very thin cigarette, suddenly said:

"Thinking about, Jack?"

"Just us," said Jack.

There was another long peaceful silence.

"Thinking about, Sam?"

"Well, Jack me boy, I was thinking we'll have to get some sort of idea what we're going to do with ourselves. Reckon we ought to have something to aim at, like getting a bit of hoot together to buy a little farm or a place to live or something. The way we've been, just knocking around, working when and where we feel like it, is about the best way a man can live. He's got time to be a man that way. But a young bloke like you should have something to work for besides just living.

"Long as it's not milking cows I don't care what we do, said Jack.

"What do you say to a little place up against the bush somewhere with a back paddock that needs the scrub clearing off it and fences that need fixing? Somewhere you can always go back to for a spell when you get tired of travelling.

"With a dog tied up and horses in the horse paddock," put in Jack, his eyes shining in the firelight.

"And a rifle and the shotgun on the kitchen wall."

"And a mantelpiece for the cartridges."

"And a woodstove and an open fire."

"And snow in the winter to keep warm in."

"And a sledge for firewood."

"And no neighbours."

"And chooks and ducks."

"And sheep and a cow for fresh milk."

"And deer and pigs in the bush."

"And a tame wild pig to eat the scraps."

"And a river with trout."

"And possums to trap."

"And boots and saddles and coats in the porch."

"And an old truck under the trees to get bits off."

"And a big leaky old shed to put things in and work in on wet days."

"But how are we going to get money to live on," said Jack, suddenly returning to their camp by the road.

"Well, a man could sell deerskins and possum tokens and posts and battens, and break in horses and breed dogs, and do odd jobs like fencing and bush work, and graze stock for cockies in the winter once you get the fences fixed up. There's plenty of ways to make a few quid. Got to get the place first."

"How much will it cost, Sam?"

"Hard to say. Might be able to lease a place for a few quid a year. Or get it for a few hundred quid down and then pay it off. Or you could buy it outright for a few thousand quid."

"Can't see us ever getting thousands of quid," said Jack soberly. "And paying it off doesn't sound as if we'll have much freedom to do what we want, does it?"

"Yeah, that's the trouble with that idea," agreed Sam flicking a cigarette butt into the fire and standing up. "Still, you never know your luck, Jack me boy. And it's something to keep your eyes open for. Anyway, you can sleep on it. Probably won't be able to recognise the place in the morning."

The morning was a cold, wet haze of drizzling rain. Their little farm was a thousand miles away. Tyres sizzled on the wet road and the windscreen wiper whined like a waterpump. Jack was surprised to notice how far away and unimportant his father's farm was now. He hardly ever thought about it these days. He rubbed a film of mist off the window and looked out to see if there was any bush and rivers.

At Hastings, three days later, they called in to see if there was any mail at Sam's friend's place. A money order for forty-seven pounds thirteen and a penny was there for them.

"That cheque must have gone through after all," said Sam in surprise. "Dan Porter must have sold a bale of dags or something."

"Don't let's argue about it," said Jack happily. "That eel soup of yours we had yesterday didn't do my appetite as much damage as I thought. I'm starving."

Jack was so hungry he didn't even notice the waitress until she brought them cups of tea.

"How's that little lot, Sam?" he asked, poking a grimy thumb towards the girl's disappearing figure.

"Hard to catch as a new-calved heifer and harder to get rid of than a wind-broken gelding," snorted Sam. "Get a man into more trouble than a wool-chasing dog. Spend all your dough, keep you in a steady job so you have to crawl to the boss, and bust you up with all your mates. Lever promises out of you that you can't keep and then call you a liar. Next thing they get you so you can't think and before you know where you are, you're married and nagged and worried, and only half a man and wondering why the hell why! No, Jack me boy, the woman caper is a crook one!"

Jack was surprised at the bitterness in Sam's words. He'd never heard him speak about anything so earnestly before. They paid their bill in silence and left the restaurant. Jack kept his eyes well clear of the waitress as she counted the change into his hand and rolled back towards the kitchen.

"You don't go the women much, Sam?" asked Jack, as they climbed into the truck and turned into the north road.

"No Jack, the way women are fixed you have to give them more than you can possibly get out of it. After a while it gets to be more than it's worth. But you're stuck with them by that time and it's too late."

"But what if you fall in love with them, Sam?"

"That's a damn sight worse than anything. All this singing and books and screeching and bellering about what a marvellous thing love is, is just a lot of tripe, Jack. I've been as much in love as a man can get and believe me, there's nothing so miserable and upsetting and lousy in the whole world. Can't work properly, can't think about anything except what the woman's up to when you're not with her, and when you are with her you're miserable because you can't stay there. You spend months wandering around like a blind horse, looking for something you're not going to get anyway. Then you think you've got it, and your head goes round like a fan-belt, and by the time it stops you're married. You start to think you're happy then, but it doesn't take long to wake up.

"I once loved a woman so much I stayed round the town she lived in for four months. Took her out a few times and one day I tells her I love her and wanted to get married. She ups and screams with laughter in my face!

"I climbed aboard the old bomb and drove off feeling like every rib in my carcase had been busted in three places. I wandered around for months, wondering what to do about it, but there's no cure except time. And a long time it takes, too. You think it's never going to end. It probably never really does.

"Once a woman gets you she hangs on like a rata. There's kids and telephones and boots off before you come into the house and you've had it! You've got as close as you can get but it's not close enough. And you can't go back and have another go at it because you're too busy telling lies to keep yourself out of trouble to even remember what being a man is like.

"No, Jack me boy, she's a grim business. I only wish you could learn from what happened to me, but you'll have to see it for yourself or it won't be real."

"But you don't have to marry them," said Jack uncertainly.

"If they want y', they'll get y'. Don't worry about that lot! They've got all the gear to do it with," answered Sam definitely.

"But all marriages aren't like that, are they, Sam?"

"No. One in about two hundred looks okay, but they're the ones who don't like blowing up in front of the visitors. When they get on their own they go it hammer and tongs to make up for lost time."

"Had an uncle and aunt who reckoned they never had rows," said Jack.

"They're either liars or they've got no guts," said Sam with certainty. "Couples bitching at each other is human nature and there's nothing anyone can do about it except remember the times when things are going smooth and forget about the rows. Money's the cause of most of it. Either there's too much or not enough. I reckon if you found a couple who had no money trouble you'd be pretty close to a happy marriage. But I've never come across it.

"If you ever want to take on a woman you've got to decide whether it's going to be worth it if she can't take the knocks and starts bitching at you. It's no good trying them out first because they can keep it up longer than you can. You'll run into married blokes who say they're pleased enough with life. But me, I'd sooner go to bed with a wet dog and cook me own tucker. The price of the smell of a roast dinner is too high for me."

Jack looked across at Sam and wondered what had happened to make him so bitter about women. He refrained from pursuing the subject and a few minutes later the old happy Sam was telling him how Uncle Wally's draught horses bolted through the road gate with the chain-harrows and galloped along the main street of Papakura with a whole swarm of wasps stinging hell out of them.

They bought a newspaper in a Napier milk bar and Sam opened it over the steering wheel of the truck.

"Scrub-cutters wanted up Puketitiri. Ten bob a chain. That's a fiver an acre. No good to us, Jack me boy. Lousiest bloody job in the country. Last resort. Let's see now — shepherd for hill

127

country station. Own dogs and saddle. — Working manager for two thousand acre sheep- and cattle-run. Nope. Ah, here's one! Men, two, for casual work on small station. Good wages and conditions. Please phone 61B or call Mrs Wagner, Homai station. What say we give this Missus Wagner a lash, Jack? If it's no good we can shove off again."

"Sounds fair enough, Sam. Know where it is?"

"No, but we'll soon find out," replied Sam, starting the truck and patting it into low gear. "I'll whip in and ask at the cop-shop. They're bound to know."

Having got directions from a painstaking, map-drawing constable, they set off on the thirty-mile drive to Mrs Wagner's Homai station.

"How long have you been knocking around country like this, Sam?" asked Jack, voicing a thought that had often occurred to him over the past few months.

"Since I was about sixteen," said Sam. After a few moments he continued, "Four days after my sixteenth birthday to be exact."

"Fair go?" asked Jack, scenting a yarn in Sam's tone.

"Yep. I'd never been more than twenty mile from Uncle Wally's farm. Left school when I was fifteen and settled down to work for him till I turned twenty-one. He was going to put me on shares on my twenty-first birthday."

"What changed your mind?" asked Jack, settling comfortably into his corner and rolling two smokes.

"It started the Sunday I turned sixteen," remembered Sam. "My young cousin Davey, who was staying with us for the holidays, had a loose tooth so I decided to operate. Sat him in a kitchen chair, tied a length of trout-cast round his tooth and on to the porch door.

"Slam! and Davey hit the door before it shut. I blindfolded him with a teatowel for the next try, but he leapt forward the first time I moved, caught his forehead a beautiful smack on the open door, and tried to tell me his tooth wasn't loose after all. I took the string off the door and led him like a prize bull down to the woolshed.

"We climbed on to the roof, and I tied a rock to the free end of Davey's string and threw it over. Davey jumped after it and broke his leg. They took him off to hospital. Didn't see why I should get all the blame for just trying to help; but I got it all the same. Spent the rest of my birthday chain-harrowing the back paddock in pouring rain.

"On Monday I caught the horses — the youngest of them was old enough to vote — and hitched them up to the only two-horse wagon in the district. Uncle Wally never missed a chance to skite about it. The old piano case on wheels creaked and splashed and rumbled across the flooded river-crossing towards the road. Had to lift my feet above the water that flowed across the rotten decking and pretended not to see the girlfriend's father drive past in their new car.

"The neighbour and I loaded the wagon with some hay Uncle Wally was buying off him and I drove slowly back down the hill, sitting on top of the load with the reins looped around the pitchfork handle. Crossing back over the river the wagon wheels chocked against some big stones that had washed down with the flood, and the horses jibbed. Even a dig in the backside with the pitchfork wouldn't stir them, and water was lapping at the bottom of the hay. It looked as though I was going to get blamed again for something that wasn't my fault. Then I got it all worked out. The day was saved! I forked a bundle of hay across on to the bank and jumped after it, took it upstream, set fire to it and threw it on the water. Then I ran back, clambered on to the load and waited for the bundle of blazing hay to scare the horses into action.

"The fire drifted closer and the horses didn't even lift their bottom lips out of the water. I shouted and shook the reins. Then I tried to hold off the bundle of burning hay but it was too late. I tried to stop the wagon catching fire but the smoke and heat drove me back till I had to climb down the wheel-spokes into the river. As soon as I let go the wagon the current got me. Climbed the bank just in time to see the horses bounce the last of Uncle Wally's wagon off the third gateway along the river flat — it was smoking like a small boy on sale day. I doused one or two fires that had sprung up round the place and went up to the house to take the blame.

"On Tuesday the Featherstones came and everything went off okay until afternoon tea. I'd left an eel in a sugar bag on the front porch and when I looked up from my cream-cake there it was, curling across the hall carpet towards the living-room door. I tried to excuse myself, but Uncle Wally said to wait until everyone was finished. Then I blew my nose and stuffed the corner of the tablecloth into my pocket with the handkerchief. In a hurry to be first to leave the table I dragged one or two things on to the floor and upset the milk jug and broke one of Aunt Sarah's wedding cups. In the confusion I tried to kick the eel out the door but it went under the piano and ended up inside it. Later I heard Uncle Wally explaining to Aunt Sarah that you don't thrash a sick dog to make it better.

"On Wednesday I finished ploughing the river paddock with the horses unscathed and the plough in one piece. I had a bath, borrowed Uncle Wally's razor for a shave I didn't need and he didn't know about, and polished up my best pair of shoes. I was going to the girlfriend's place for tea and to play cards by the fire, and maybe for a walk if the weather was okay. For a whole week I'd been working out what to say and how and when to say it. Tonight was the big night.

"In one of Uncle Wally's detachable-collar shirts, one of his old patterned ties, my best grey trousers, and the sports coat Uncle Bert left behind him, I stood back from the big mirror to have a look at myself. Tried out various positions and expressions but none of them went with the clothes. It was no good saying important things in clothes like that. If only I had a new suit like Uncle Wally's.

"It was hanging slightly apart from the rest of his gear in the other half of the wardrobe. A shiny, sharp, brand-new, pin-striped suit. The idea scared me a bit — and if I waited till they were in bed it'd make me too late. I went to the door and listened. They were sitting round the wireless in the living room. It was just a matter of sneaking out the front door. I went into the bathroom and plastered my hair down with plenty of hair-oil. Listened for a bit, closed the bedroom door and got out the suit. I stood there smelling it for a while. Still hadn't dared make up my mind to really do it. I held the coat up in front of me. It looked beaut. Then I took off the sports coat and threw it under the bed, dragged the suit trousers on over the others and dived into the coat. Looked into the mirror and saw that it was worth the risk and quickly switched off the light.

"I got safely away in the old Ford I'd bought off a Maori joker at a sale. I saw that in the hurry to get away I'd forgotten to change the sticking plaster on a cut on my finger and it was a bit ragged and dirty on it, so I stopped and took it off. The cut looked worse than the plaster, so I wound it on again. It wouldn't stick properly but I decided to keep my hand in my pocket or the finger folded in. I practised shoving my shoulders forward so the coat sleeves didn't hang over my hands. The length of the strides didn't matter because they hid the ones beneath and partly covered my shoes.

"When I got there everyone was in the lounge. They had a dirty big fire going. It was so hot that sweat and hair-oil was running down my face and neck in little creeks before I'd been there ten minutes. Mister Holdson kept building up the fire and saying how it looked as if winter was coming early that year. And I kept saying, yeah it did, didn't it, and thinking about the handkerchief in the pocket of that sports coat I'd thrown under my bed back home.

" 'New suit, son?' says Mister Holdson.

" 'Yeah,' says I, wondering if he'd mention it to Uncle Wally at the sale next day.

"Then their dog came in. A snarly, snapping, overfed little ratbag of a thing called Buttons. One of them Pomeranians. It must have found out I didn't like it much because it sat under a chair snarling at me all night. Every time I moved Buttons started barking and snapping at me. The girlfriend reckoned it would be all right once it got to know me. But it never got the chance. I sat there lousing up games of five hundred and wiping sweat and hair-oil on the sleeve of Uncle Wally's coat till Mister Holdson said it was time we were all getting off to bed.

"Then I asked the girlfriend if she wanted to come down to the tip with me the next day, shooting rats with shanghais.

"Missus Holdson said, 'Well I never!' Mister Holdson coughed and the girlfriend started to say something and then stopped.

"I could see something had gone wrong so I left.

"They'd let Buttons out to use the garden and I met him on the corner of the house on my way out to my truck. I don't know how it happened, Jack — but my foot just shot out and punted that dear little puppy fair into the passionfruit trellis, about thirty feet away. Then I bolted for the truck for a fast getaway but I flooded her and sat there grinding at the starter while all the Holdsons fluttered around their screaming little dog just up the path. The only time the Model A ever let me down.

"I stopped for a think on the way home because it was early and Uncle Wally might not be asleep yet. Walked the last hundred yards to the house and crept through the little side gate, lifting my feet high so as not to get drops of dew on Uncle Wally's pants. I walked on the grass to avoid crunching on the gravel path, and sneaked round the back of the house so I wouldn't have to pass under Uncle Wally's bedroom window. On the last corner before the back door I trod fair on the edge of a roasting-dish full of waste oil that I'd drained from the sump of my truck. It flipped up and slopped oil all over the front of that beautiful suit.

"At half-past two the next morning, Jack me boy, I left home. The difference between a sick dog and a bloke who's just ruined Uncle Wally's new suit was a bit too distinguishable altogether. Left a note saying I'd decided to go on a holiday and haven't heard from Uncle Wally since.

"That was about thirty years ago and I haven't come across anything yet that's better than travelling around the place, working when you feel like it or have to. And no one to explain to when you get yourself into trouble. You can't beat it."

MRS WAGNER

It was dusking into a cold, windy evening when Sam nosed the Ford through a road gate that bore a rotting sign saying: "Homai Station", "Please close the Gate" and "We use the Bevin Harrow" on it.

"These women are either very good or absolutely rotten to work for," said Sam, as Jack climbed back into the cab after closing the gate. "If we find her skinning a dead ram she'll be one of the good ones."

"What'll she be doing if she's one of the crook ones?" asked Jack.

"Looking through the curtains to see who's coming," answered Sam.

Mrs Wagner wasn't looking through the curtains — but she wasn't skinning a dead ram either. It was a ewe.

They parked the truck beside a Land Rover by the house and went up to where a heavily-built, middle-aged woman, dressed like a man, was hanging a sheepskin over a gate that opened into the yards.

"Missus Wagner?" asked Sam, in the voice Jack knew he reserved exclusively for women.

"That's right. What can I do for you?"

"Saw your ad in the paper and came out to see about the job," said Sam.

"Oh yes. Well, you'd better come down to the house. I don't suppose you've eaten yet?"

"Matter of fact we haven't," said Sam and Jack together.

"Well, we'll see what we can rake up for you. I had my tea half an hour ago."

Jack thought to himself that to catch a sheep and kill, skin and clean it in half an hour wasn't bad going. Missus Wagner evidently knew what she was doing. She led them down to the house and into the kitchen.

On a table in the middle of the floor was a drenching-gun, a quarter of mutton, a packet of Cooper's Arsenical Sheep Dip Powder, a broken bridle, two dog collars, a pile of *Journals of Agriculture*, a tin of Stockholm tar, a pair of footrot shears, a piece of manuka and a partly-dismantled chainsaw. A ewe with two lambs was tied to one of the table legs by a front foot. An old army rifle rusted quietly away in a corner and four staple boxes, covered with sacks and sheepskins, served as chairs. The cooking and eating was apparently done in a small pantry just off the kitchen, where a stove smoked and glowed under two steaming pots.

While Mrs Wagner cooked them a meal of mutton chops, mashed potatoes and tinned peas, Sam dragged a box up to the table and began poking about with the chainsaw. Jack picked up another box that looked as though it had fallen over, found a possum curled up under it and quickly put it back again. Choosing another, he sat beside Sam.

"What's wrong with it, Sam?"

"Starter-rope pulled out. Have to strip the things half to bits to get them back in."

The job was nearly completed when Mrs Wagner brought in two plates of food, put one on the pile of *Journals of Agriculture*, the other on the packet of Cooper's Arsenical Sheep Dip Powder, and told them to get stuck in.

"Have you had any experience with sheep and cattle work?" she asked.

"Yeah," said Sam. "Years of it."

"Twelve-ten a week and your tucker suit you?"

"Yeah, that'll do us," said Sam through a mouthful of potato. And they were employed.

They slept that night in a front room that was used for storing bales of hay and several thousand other things, and moved next day into a pleasant little two-roomed bach, two hundred yards away from the house.

Mrs Wagner had been living on her own for six years. The place carried five thousand sheep and two hundred head of cattle on four and a half thousand acres, and the lambing was nearly finished. The river was full of trout and the fences were in a shocking mess. Mrs Wagner attended to the stock while Sam and Jack split posts, battens and strainers and began patching up some of the more important fences. In the evenings they sat in their hut talking about things.

"Y'know, Sam," said Jack, on a perfect evening, "a man could do worse than stay here for a few months."

A look flicked into Sam's eyes that Jack didn't quite understand.

"It's not too bad," he agreed, after a moment. "Missus Wagner's a bit of a beaut, isn't she."

"She's a hard case all right. Seen her bedroom?"

"No. What's it like?"

"There's a photo of her riding a steer at a show and more junk than in the kitchen."

Sam laughed.

"She's not the tidiest hunk of work I've come across, but the old girl's got a heart of gold. Give you the shirt off her back before she'd see you stuck."

"Did you see her throw that strainer over the fence for me yesterday? You'd think it was a batten the way she handled it."

"Last bloke she had working here left because she smacked him in the kisser for kicking one of her dogs, the old roadman told me yesterday."

"Oh, she won't take any funny business. You'd be going for it to put one across Alice Wagner. But treat her okay and she'll give you a fair enough deal. Uncle Wally had a close go with a herd-tester like that."

Jack pounced on the infant yarn. "Yeah? What happened, Sam?"

"Monstrous hunk of work she was — Bessie Gray — stood about twenty-four hands and a guts on 'er like a politician. She used to come creaking up the hill on a horse and buggy, swearing like nobody's business because the horse wouldn't trot and she was late. Then she'd sit up half the night bellowing at Uncle Wally about the neighbours' kids giving cheek.

"In the cowshed old Bessie spilt buckets of milk everywhere and roared at Uncle Wally and the cows till Uncle Wally started getting nervous and the cows held their milk. After a couple of days we were pretty glad to see Bessie heave herself into her buggy and bully the old horse into a staggering trot towards the neighbour with the cheeky kids.

"Once, when Uncle Wally was opening the road gate for her, the horse got a bit bad-tempered and reared up in the shafts. Bessie tried to get out of the cart and fell on to the road. So did a gallon jar of sulphuric acid. She bounced, but the jar didn't. It smashed on a rock and splashed all over her. She took her overalls off and stood there in the biggest pair of bloomers you ever saw in your life, cracking the overalls like a stockwhip. Uncle Wally and I managed to hang on to the horse till the acid that Bessie was flicking everywhere started stinging it. It suddenly took off and scattered us and Bessie's gear and a chain of new fence all over our hay paddock.

"The sight of her lumbering after the horse in those enormous bloomers, and swearing like a teamster was too much for Uncle Wally. He started screaming with laughter. Bessie gave up chasing the horse and took to Uncle Wally. Ran him along the fence and into a big raupo swamp. She plunged in after him and, Jack me boy, you won't believe this, but she flattened a good half-acre of the thickest raupo you ever saw in your life. Pukekos, wild ducks and quail diving off in all directions. And Bessie up to her knees in mud and swearing to throttle Uncle Wally when she got her hands on him. Uncle Wally's gumboots had filled up with water and mud and he only just managed to keep in front, yelling for me to go and get someone. But there was no one to get.

"There was a steep hill on the far side of the swamp and I thought Uncle Wally was going to have a go at climbing it, but he doubled back into the paddock. His gumboots were so heavy that he couldn't even bend his knees but Bessie was tiring by this time. She came up out of that swamp like one of those prehistoric monsters. Strides half down and covered with red mud. She sat on the bank gasping like a water pump and saying: 'That's the finish! Never again!' She was too stonkered to swear any more. Uncle Wally was over by the gate taking his boots off when Bessie stood up. As soon as she moved he grabbed the boot he had off and ran again, like a pheasant with a broken wing, to put a bit more distance between them.

"Bessie and I collected her gear and caught the horse. I fixed up a few bits of broken harness while she took her suitcase across to the cowshed to clean herself up and put some clothes on. Uncle Wally didn't come back from the bull paddock till she'd disappeared round the corner half a mile up the road. Reckoned he was going to get the police on to her for assault and wrecking his fence, but he never got round to it."

"Did Bessie ever come back again, Sam?" asked Jack.

"No, Jack me boy. She didn't even finish her rounds. Next time a new herd-tester came. Had a little car, this one. A different sort altogether. She tried to convert Uncle Wally to a Jehovah's Witness but he told her he was Social Credit and wasn't thinking of changing. She was reasonably harmless. It's the Bessies you've got to watch, Jack. I don't reckon Missus Wagner would be much easier to handle once you got her started. And a woman's more dangerous than a man because you can't hit them back. They're vicious, Jack, but this one won't give us any trouble we don't ask for.

"What's the time? Strike, it's ten o'clock! About time we hit the pit. Pass me going-to-bed pants, Jack me boy, and I won't hit you when I'm drunk."

Many of what Jack was to think about as "the good old days" followed one another in Mrs Wagner's ugly little valley. Sam's instruction gave him confidence in a hundred back-country jobs that are studiously avoided by the people who peddle correspondence courses. And he learned a lot more than the jobs themselves — Sam was teaching him how to be a man.

Confident and happy, he grabbed a handpiece and made a rough but promising job of shearing his first sheep; by the time he'd shorn a hundred he was really getting the hang of it. Because he knew Sam wasn't going to blow up on him if he made a mistake, he did a good breaking-in job on one of Mrs Wagner's colts, with Sam only helping and advising now and then. He shod the pack-horse. He mustered the hoggets off the back paddock on his own; all of them.

He hung gates and fixed things he hardly knew anything about. He made his own flies and caught trout in the river to smoke in their new smoke-house on the river-bank. He killed and dressed the fattest wether in the killing paddock when it was his turn. He listened to a thousand of Sam's yarns, and believed every word of them. He spliced ropes that didn't need splicing and rolled them under his foot like Sam did. He read out the bits from the paper that Sam would have read out if he'd got it first. He said things Sam would have said and even tried his hand at telling an occasional yarn.

Good or bad, happy or "brassed-off", working or loafing, Sam was Jack's idea of a real man.

Sam's yarns dried up a bit after a visit to town but Jack supposed it was because he was running short and had to spread them out a bit. And if Sam went all quiet now and again Jack didn't worry about it. He knew it wouldn't be long before everything was all right.

One afternoon, when they were spending a few hours at the Paparoa pub and Sam was outside, a drunk Maori caught Jack staring at him and staggered over with a look on his face that Jack didn't care for in the least.

"Who the hell do you think you're staring at?" he demanded, pushing Jack in the shoulder.

The bar was suddenly silent and Jack knew the Maori was going to hit him in exactly the amount of time it took him to swing his fist, when Sam said from the door:

"Jack! Cut that out!"

He came over and got between Jack and the Maori.

"Look here, Jack, you know what happened last time, don't you? Want to end up in jail again?" Sam turned to the bewildered Maori.

"For God's sake, mate, don't let him start anything. He'll murder the lot of us if he gets going!" He lowered his voice confidentially. "This is Jack Wilson. He got kicked out of the ring for doing his block. He's okay when he's sober but when he's got a few in he goes berko. Just out of jail for half killing a bloke in a pub up Gisborne way. Poor coot was just standing there having a quiet beer, and smack! Jack turns round and takes to 'im. Took six of us to drag him off. Now you just ignore him and walk up to the other end of the bar. I'll try and get him out of here."

140

He gave the Maori, who'd sobered considerably in the past few minutes, an urgent shove, so that he crept as far along the bar as he could and got behind a group of his mates, who had developed a sudden and absorbing interest in their beer and their own business. Sam took Jack by the arm as though he was a homicidal maniac and gently led him to the door, saying cheerfully:

"To hell with this place, Jack. We'll shoot through to the next pub, shall we?"

Behind them an excited babble broke out in the bar.

"That was a close go," said Sam, reaching for the starter button. "It's no good trying to talk sense to that sort of joker once he takes a set on you. You'll have more mates than you know what to do with after that, though."

"Don't know that I'm too keen on having someone like that for a mate," said Jack nervously.

"Oh, they'll be all right from now on," said Sam.

"I remember pulling a stunt like that on a gang of shearers who thought I'd swiped a dozen of beer off them, just because I had a dozen under my foot. I did such a good job on them that I didn't have to pay for a drink all day. It back-fired on me a bit at a party they took me to that night though. Some of them came in to where I was doing a fast line with one of their women and said that some gate-crashing bush-whackers had picked on one of their blokes and it looked like a real donnie coming up. I went outside and there they were, lined up in two rows and just about ready to get stuck into it. Somebody said: 'Here's Sam Cash,' as if I was Jack Dempsey himself and everyone shut up, wondering who the hell Sam Cash was.

"I tell you, Jack me boy, I was a worried man just then. There were some tough rags in that little bunch. One king-hit and I was a goner."

"Hell Sam! What did you do?"

"I walked right into that crowd of bushmen as if they were dogs and wandered among them, looking them fair in the face, one after the other. It was so quiet you could have heard a fist close. Had to keep my thumbs hooked in my belt to stop my hands shaking. Then I walked right up to one of the most dangerous-looking roosters I've ever seen in my life and said very quietly:

" 'This'd be the best scrapper among you bunch of ratbags, wouldn't it?'

"Two or three of them said, yes, and they all stood back out of the way.

" 'Okay,' I said, 'take a swipe. I'll deal with your holler-gutted mates later. And I've got some good men watching my back, so you're on your own!'

"We stood there lookin' at each other for about a minute. Then he dropped his head, mumbled something about having 'no grudge on you personally' and sloped off. His mates started straggling back towards their truck, and the shearers all swarmed around me, patting me on the back and saying what a hard man I was. In a couple of weeks it was all round the district that I'd cleaned up a whole gang of bushmen on my own. But I wouldn't like to try that sort of thing too often. It's a pretty touchy business, making a man back out of a scrap in front of his mates. You've got to know just when to stop. If you push him too far he gets so desperate he'd sooner take a hiding than look like a coward. It only takes one good swipe and you've got no more life expectancy than a dog-tucker ram.

"And remember, Jack me boy, there's no winners in a fight. Everyone gets hurt, one way or another, and it proves absolutely nothing. Just because a man makes a bigger mess of you than you make of him doesn't prove he's a better bloke. He's usually worse. A real mate isn't going to judge you on how good you are in a knuckle-up.

"Ah — home sweet home. Open the gate for us, Jack me boy, and I won't tell Missus Wagner how you backed out of a fight with that tiny little Maori joker."

THE WAY
THE TRUCK TURNS

Life at Mrs Wagner's continued pleasantly for another few weeks before the blow fell.

Jack was working on a drafting-gate that wasn't swinging properly, when Sam came through the woolshed and sat on the rail beside him.

"Have a smoke, Jack," he said, passing him a battered tin of tobacco.

"Ta," said Jack, hitching himself up on the rail beside Sam.

"Been thinking it's about time I shoved off, Jack."

Jack's foot slipped off the bottom rail of the race. He recovered himself and said, "But why, Sam? Don't you like it here?"

"Oh it's a fair enough place to live all right. But I never stay long in one place anyway. I like to move around a bit."

"But Sam," said Jack, dismayed. "This is our little farm! I know there's no porch with saddles and oilskins, but we could fix that up. It may not be ours but . . ."

"If we stay here it will be ours," interrupted Sam. "The old girl's put the hard word on me."

"The hard word?"

"Yeah. Wants us to get married and go shares in the place."

Jack's other foot slipped off the rail.

"Get married!"

"Yeah. Have to shove off. Told her I was going. She said to ask you if you'd stay on and help with the sheep till she can get someone."

"That means we have to split up?"

"Looks like it. Can't leave the old girl in the cart. It's the only decent thing we can do."

"But what about us?"

"That's nothin' much," said Sam, looking away towards the river. "We're getting to depend on each other a bit too much

145

anyway. A man's only half a man when he can't live on his own. And you'll want to get married one day, but you won't have a chance hanging round with me like this. Y'see, Jack, I know I'll never be able to stop wandering around and it's not the sort of thing I want to drag a mate into. It's a disease, Jack."

Jack got down off the rail.

"Are you sick of me, Sam?"

"No," answered Sam, in a way that told Jack he wasn't. "If you like I'll buy your share of the truck. You can get a better one next time you go to town."

"But I don't want a better one!"

"There's a four hundred quid cheque for you down at the house, Jack me boy," said Sam, punching him gently in the arm. "You're better off with your dough in something you can use than have it sitting in a bank. Now, come and give me a hand to load my gear on the truck."

In a miserable silence Jack helped Sam find and load his gear. Sam climbed in.

"Why don't you stay the night and leave in the morning, Sam?"

"No, Jack. Makes it tougher that way."

"Which way are you going?"

"The way the truck turns when I reach the road."

"I'll come and open the gate for you."

"It's open. There's been nothing in the road paddock for two weeks."

Sam shoved his hand through the window.

"Goodbye, Jack me boy. You're a good mate."

Unbelieving, Jack shook hands with Sam. He played his last card as Sam started the truck: "You've forgotten the shotgun!"

"No I haven't. It's yours. I won't be needing it. And don't forget to put the wadding in the next lot of cartridges you make up," he added, grinning.

"Goodbye, Sam."

"Hooray, Jack. Don't forget; never tell them you can't do it."

Jack ran to the top of the hill to see which way the truck took Sam.

West, towards hills where they hadn't been yet. He walked slowly down to the hut. He hated Mrs Wagner just then.

For a week Jack mechanically did what most needed doing around the station. He saw Mrs Wagner in the distance a few times but didn't even answer her wave. He was very unhappy. Trees and wind and grass and the river reminded him of Sam. He imagined Sam telling yarns and finding new places and pulling up for a beer at a little pub on a strange road.

On a still Sunday morning he looked up from a stockwhip he was putting a new lash on and saw Mrs Wagner coming up from the house, towards where he was sitting in the doorway of his hut. She stood in one of Sam's footprints in the mud that he'd been saving and said:

"Hullo Jack. I saw you down by the river yesterday. I waved out but you didn't see me."

Jack didn't look up.

"Did Sam tell you why he left?" she asked quietly.

"Yep." He gave the new lash a hard pull to test it.

"Do you miss him, Jack?"

"Nope."

"I've got over four hundred pounds for you and I'm going in to town tomorrow. I thought you might like to come and cash your cheque."

"No — it doesn't matter — thanks."

"I thought you'd want to get that truck they're advertising in the paper. It's the same model as the one you and Sam had. If you're going to catch up with him you'll have to get a move on."

Jack looked up quickly.

"What about the work?" he asked.

"Oh, there's no need to worry about that," she said. "Things will be pretty quiet until the dipping and I can manage that. Now how about coming down to the house for a feed, Jack me boy. I've gone and cooked too much for me to handle."

Jack stood up, gave the stockwhip a flick and fell into step beside Mrs Wagner. He trod in another of Sam's old footprints.

The next afternoon Jack climbed into his new truck and shook hands with Mrs Wagner through the window.

"Goodbye, Missus Wagner. Thanks for everything."

"Good luck, Jack me boy," she said softly. "You'll find him soon. Anyone will be able to tell you if Sam's been past."

She stood back with a little wave and Jack patted the truck into low gear the way Sam did.

SORRY, MATE

"Seen a long skinny bloke in a green truck who tells yarns and can do anything, mate?"

"Nope. Sorry, mate."

"Any of you blokes know Sam Cash?"

"No. What does he look like?"

"Long and skinny. Drives a green V-8 fifteen-hundredweight and tells yarns. He has a deep voice and can do anything."

"Sorry, mate."

"Nope. Hasn't been here."

"No. Don't think so."

"Do you think I've got nothing to do except sit here all day watching the colour of the V-8s that go past?"

"Sorry, mate. Can't help you."

"Nope. Never heard of him."

"Never heard of him, mate. Sounds like a proper bastard."

"Oh, yeah. That bloke! He's working up at Stan Foster's. What colour did you say his truck was?"

"Green."

"Can't be him. This bloke's got a Chev, and it's red."

"Sorry, mate."

"No. Can't say I have."

"What name did you say, son?" asked an old man who was driving an old cow along an old country road in Taranaki.

"Sam Cash."

"Nope. Thought for a minute you might be after a bloke called Harvey Wilson who came through here a while back."

"That's him!" said Jack excitedly. "He uses that name some-times. Where did he go?"

"Couldn't say, son. Might pay you to drop in and see Joe Farnley, third place on the left up here. This Harvey Wilson bloke stayed there a couple of days I think. Didn't make himself too popular by the sound of things either."

Joe Farnley came out on his porch as Jack opened the yard gate.

"How y' goin'?" he said.

"Not bad, thanks," said Jack. "I'm looking for a bloke called Harvey Wilson. They tell me you might be able to help me."

"Harvey Wilson, eh," said Mr Farnley. "So am I. Do you know him?"

"I think it might be a mate I've been looking for all over the place."

"If I was you I'd give him up, lad. That's if it's the same joker. He's a fair dinkum rotter."

"He tells yarns," said Jack defensively.

"Yarns!" cried Mr Farnley. "Yarns! I'll tell you a yarn, and this is a true one. This Harvey Wilson character pulled in here about three weeks ago in a flash car. Reckoned he was a marine biologist. Said they were working on a new prevention dose for rickets and thought they had just the thing. He showed me a gallon of the stuff, last one he had. Herring-livers and cortisone he said it was. You inject it into the blood-stream of an in-lamb ewe and three generations of its lambs are immune from rickets. He said the stuff cost over forty quid a gallon to make but he was going round the country selling it to farmers in different districts for twenty quid a gallon, to see how it worked under different conditions and types of sheep.

"I bought this tin of stuff off him and he told me to bring in ten ewes and leave them in the woolshed overnight for him to demonstrate with. He stayed here that night and drank nearly a full bottle of my whisky. Next day he got out of bed about half-past eleven, ate half the tucker I'd got in for the weekend and then we went down to inject some of this herring-liver and stuff into the ewes.

"He showed me how to cut the veins in their ears and squirt a few drops of this stuff into the bloodstream with a hypodermic.

"He was in a bit of a hurry to get away after we'd turned the ewes out; and not much wonder. I took some of his herring-liver and stuff in to the vet to get it tested and yesterday they rang up to say it was ordinary varnish. I was thinking of getting the police on to the swine but he'll probably be miles away by this time."

"Did it kill the sheep?" asked Jack.

"No, but it made them awful sick," replied Joe Farnley. "A man that'd do that to an animal just to get a few quid wants a good swift kick in the backside and locking up for a few years."

"I don't think it can be my mate," said Jack. "He wouldn't do a thing like that."

"I should think not," said Mr Farnley. "A thieving mongrel like that wouldn't have any mates. I should have woken up to him earlier. If he'd done half the things he reckoned he'd done he'd be about two hundred and fifty years old."

"What did he look like, Mister Farnley?"

"Well, it'd be pretty hard to describe him, son. Not tall, not short, not skinny, not fat. Ordinary face, hair going grey. You know the type. There's hundreds of blokes who look like that about."

"Did he say which way he was going?"

"Yeah, he said he was going down to Wellington to supervise the laying of a cable across Cook Strait."

"Well thanks a lot, Mr Farnley."

"You're welcome, lad. If you happen to run across the Harvey Wilson who sold me that tin of varnish I'd appreciate to know where he hangs out. Box 209, Eltham, is the address."

"Okay, I'll do that," said Jack absently.

As he drove away, Jack remembered how Mrs Wagner had said: "Anyone will be able to tell you if Sam's been past." He drove south towards Wellington but never picked up the trail of the Harvey Wilson who sold the tin of varnish to Joe Farnley again. He turned off at Palmerston North and travelled up the east coast to have a look round Tolaga Bay and Opotiki. He found no trace of Sam Cash — or Harvey Wilson.

After two months of searching Jack had to get a job with a gang of forestry workers because he had no money left. None of them had heard of Sam Cash.

Three months of pruning the lower branches off young pine trees saw Jack with a gutful of forestry and forestry workers and enough money to continue his search for a long skinny bloke in a green truck, who told yarns in a deep voice and could do anything.

The only clue he had as to where Sam was, was the knowledge that he wouldn't be anywhere he'd been before. He worked his way through the Wairarapa, asking the same questions and getting the same answers.

"Sorry, mate."

"Nope. Can't help you."

"Sorry, mate."

"Sorry, mate."

A rabbitter's wife on the coast road at Akitio thought he was asking for money and chased him off the place with a slasher.

A month after that he called in to the Upper Hutt police station.

"No, can't help you at all, lad. The best thing to do is look on the Electoral Roll."

"Oh, no," said Jack. "Sam wouldn't put his name on that on principle."

"Wouldn't he just," said the constable, grabbing a pencil. "What did you say his name was?"

"Harvey Wilson," said Jack. And fled.

At Awakino he followed the trail of a "hard-case bloke called Sam" for four days. The bloke's name turned out to be Dan, and he wasn't very pleased with Jack because he'd thought it was the police he'd been dodging.

At Kawhia a roadman swore he'd been talking to Sam the day before.

"A long skinny bloke, m'boy? Yeah, that'll be him. Green truck with a big dent in the mudguard. That's him all right. Said he'd been in the Rawleighs business for two years. Had his wife and kiddie with him . . ."

As the months added themselves up towards a year, Jack gradually lost heart. He'd travelled eighteen thousand miles, looking for a long skinny bloke in a green truck, who told yarns and could do anything. He took a job wheeling barrows of concrete along planks on the new Waikato dam. He worked at Meremere, stripping the boxing off concrete work. He painted huts at Waipa. At Kaingaroa he told them he could drive a bulldozer, and then got the sack because he couldn't even start one. He asked his old question less and less frequently.

At Taupo he got a job clearing sections for a building contractor. He worked with a bloke called Tom, who'd been all round the world and talked about it so much that Jack had given up trying to get a word in on the conversations and just listened. Even when Tom asked him a question he'd answer it himself before Jack could open his mouth.

One night they went to a party that got thoroughly out of control and when they turned up to work after lunch the next day they got a week's notice as well as the rough edge of the builder's tongue. That afternoon, lying in the shade of a path of manuka that should have been cut two days before, Tom suddenly said, "Y'know, Jack, you remind me of a bloke I worked with for a while last year. Don't know why because he was about twice your age."

Jack sat up. "What . . .?" he began.

"Sam somebody or other. Can't remember his other name off hand."

"Was it — Cash?"

"Might have been. Couldn't be sure now."

"Where . . .?"

"Well, it was around the beginning of last year when I first ran into Sam. The swamp between the old Otau mill and the bush was dried up and we'd put in a few culverts and got a stockpile of logs on the skids. The job was way behind schedule and everybody was going eyes out to get the mill going again, and one afternoon Sam came sloping up the road. I remember how his strides hung so low that the backs of the cuffs scraped on the road when he walked. His hat flopped over his face so he had to stick his chin out to see properly. He'd been on the booze and finished up the night before on a bottle of meths or Aussie whisky or something.

"He sorted out the boss and told him it would cost him seven-and-six to give him an hour's trial as mill manager. We were just about full up at the time and it was going to be a couple of days before the mill was going properly anyway — but Sam still got his hour's trial. He rubbed out his smoke between his finger and thumb, put the butt in his pocket and came over to where I'd been trying to get a piece of belting the right length to go over two of the pulleys before I cut and joined it. He threw the belt over one pulley, then the other and, after looking at it for a few seconds, he

155

marked a place with his thumb and cut it through with the axe. While he was over scattering "useless" gear from the saw-doctor's kit among the sawdust and setting and sharpening the breaking-down saw with a pair of fencing pliers and a file, I joined the belt and found that the tension between the two pulleys was exactly right.

"By this time the boss was looking a bit worried as if he wasn't quite sure what he'd let himself in for. Sam never hurried when he did a thing but he seemed to make everyone go like hell just by being there and in a few hours everything was just about ready for the first log to go through the saw.

"Sam stood rolling a smoke at the lever that would bring a big rimu log down on to the saw and the boss nodded to him. Sam threw the lever and walked away lighting his smoke. It looked like the saw was going to jam and buckle in the log because it was heading down the rails twice as fast as it should have been. Everybody ran to watch and the boss dived across to switch off the motors, but that log was lined up perfectly; it went through the saw as easy as the hundreds Sam sent after it. He fished a rule out of his hip pocket and threw it to the boss, who measured both ends of the log and installed Sam as his permanent mill manager.

"Sam was the sort of bloke a man could really work for. He had a way of telling you to do a thing that made you feel good about being asked to do it. And he never done his block about anything that went wrong. Once when the tractor-driver came down and told Sam he couldn't get his tractor off the side of the hill without tipping it over, Sam went up and tied the winch rope back on to a stump, locked the top track and let her rip with the winch going at the same time. He drove that nine-ton tractor straight up a hill that you could hardly walk up. None of us had any idea that Sam could even drive a tractor before that.

"One day Sam told the boss to keep out of the mill except on business because it put the blokes off with him hanging around all the time. And the boss did; we were putting out half as much timber again as the bigger mill down the river.

"Then one morning when we were just getting started up and the first log of the day was in the flitches, Sam switched off the motors and asked who was coming into town with him to pick up a cheque. We all had a month's pay coming to us so nobody stayed at the camp. We hobnailed into the office behind Sam and collected our dough.

"Down town we congregated in the boozer. Sam was as good at drinking as he was at running a mill. He drank us all under the table and carried on soaking up beer with a couple of Maori blokes who were short of a few bob.

"By late afternoon the rest of us had had a feed and were coming right again so quite a bit of grog was bought for the evening session. Sam had to be booted out of the pub when it closed and was slightly red in the face after six hours on the booze, but he'd got hold of two bottles of crook whisky and was in no mood for stopping. Once Sam got hold of a bottle of grog he had no time to eat or sleep or get drunk.

"All the boys wanted to get back to camp, but Sam decided to go round and see a bloke he knew who lived over the other side of town, so we ended up in this joker's sitting-room. We launched an attack on the beer, but things didn't go off too well. It was the way Sam drank. Not like an ordinary bloke, but as if he was going to kick the bucket if he didn't pour as much whisky down his throat as his stomach would leave. In the finish we had to leave him behind and go back to camp without him.

"Work at the mill was late and in a proper mess next day. We all kept watching for Sam to come up the road but he never showed. The boss came up to the cookhouse that night and told us that Sam had been round the office demanding more money and threw in the job when he didn't get it.

"The job was pretty dead without Sam, and one by one we left for better-sounding work. I ended up on a construction job at Murupara, and it was there that I heard about him again.

He'd been caught towing a bloke's car through Tokoroa with a converted Ministry of Works grader in the middle of the night. Drunk as a skunk he was. Reckoned the grader was public property and he had as much right to use it as anyone else. His lawyer walked out of the courtroom when Sam told the beak he didn't actually have a job but he was thinking of getting one as a grader-driver the next day. They stuck him in jail for two years. It seems Sam had run out on his missus and owed hundreds of quid in maintenance. He had a prohibition order out against him too. A waster and a vagabond the beak said. But of course he never saw Sam bringing a log through the breaking-down saw or watched him lining up the flitches on the bench, or scarfing a leaning matai so it twisted on the stump as it fell and all the big branches were on top of the log. He never knew the Sam we knew.

"I suppose they can't help it, but they lost a lot of good timber when they dumped old Sam in Mount Crawford — hey! Where you going, Jack?"

"Mount Crawford," yelled Jack, slamming the door of his truck. He heard Tom shouting something to him but he didn't wait to find out what it was.

"Where's Mount Crawford?" asked Jack, diving through the door of the Taupo police station.

"You'll find out quick enough if you come charging in here without knocking, young feller. Look at your boots. Go out and wipe some of that mud off them."

Jack went back to the door and wiped his boots.

"Now, me lad, what do you want?"

"Mount Crawford! Just found out my mate's in there."

"What do you expect me to do about it?"

"I just want to know where it is."

"Wellington."

Jack dashed out to his truck.

"Hey! You!"

Jack stopped and looked round.

"Yes you!" said the sergeant. "You've kicked the mat right off my porch. What's the idea?"

"Sorry," said Jack, coming back and putting the mat back.

"If you drive like you run you'll be lucky to ever see that mate of yours. Now you take it easy, m'lad."

Jack collected his pay and drove all night.

HANG ON A MINUTE MATE

"You'll have to come back at two o clock on Saturday," said the warden. "There's no visiting during the week."

"But I've come all the way from Taupo," said Jack desperately.

"Sorry. Two o'clock on Saturday." And the little hole in the door clapped shut like a guillotine.

He slept in the front of his truck that night and went round to the police station in the morning.

"Yes, what is it?" asked a lazing constable.

"My mate's in jail at Mount Crawford."

"Good! Probably belongs there."

"I was wondering if he could be let out."

"Were you now?"

"Yes."

"Well, he can't."

"Is there anyone who lets people off?"

"Yeah — God. Now clear out of here. We're busy."

On Saturday, at two o'clock, Jack was let into a room inside the jail with a small crowd of other visitors. He signed his name and who he wanted to visit in a big book. Sam Cash.

Then they were led into a long room with long stools and long wire-netting. He was very nervous.

Prisoners started filing into the other side of the room. Soon he was the only visitor who didn't have a prisoner to talk to. He asked the warder on the door if Sam Cash was coming.

The warder spoke to another warder.

The other warder went away and came back. He said something to the first warder, who called Jack over.

"Cash isn't seeing anyone," he said.

Jack was stunned.

"But did you tell him it was Jack Lilburn?"

"Yes. No visitors, he says, and no visitors it is. This chap here will show you out."

"But — will you take a message to him. Tell him . . ."

"Sorry. We can't take messages."

And the other warder escorted Jack out to the front gates.

"What'd 'e want, Sammy?" asked Scotty, glancing at a warder who was locking the gate of the exercise yard behind himself. Sam sat beside Scotty against the wall.

"Visitor wanted to see me," he said. "Bloke I was knocking around with for a while. Lend us a smoke, Jock, and I'll pay you back Thursday."

Scotty passed his tobacco, saying, "Ain't you goin' out to 'ave a yarn with 'im, Sammy?"

"No, not worth it."

"No-hoper?"

"Aw, not really, Jock. He's just a young bloke. Jack somebody or other. Well-meaning sort of a joker but a bit young and silly on it. Always lousing things up. I remember the first time I seen young Jack. I was driving a bulldozer in a quarry up Ararimu way and one day the boss brought up this new powder-monkey and said for me to show him where we wanted the face blasted. I pointed out the outcrop we'd been working on and then went back to my tractor to read my paper.

"I noticed the young bloke digging a big hole in the ground and thought it must be some new-fangled way of blasting. Then he dropped a plug of gelly, a detonator and half a coil of fuse into the hole. I sat up to watch this and the young feller went out of sight round the corner. Then he came running back with a double page of newspaper blazing in his hand, plunged it into the hole and tore past me yelling, 'Run for it!' He'd never seen a stick of gelignite in his life.

"The boss came up to see what was going on. He had a look in the hole and sacked the young bloke on the spot. I thought it was so funny I couldn't help laughing so I got the sack too. I offered young Jack a lift into town in my Model A and by the time we got there we were teamed up and heading down the line looking for jobs, but not very hard.

"We had ten quid to go before we were broke so we drove round looking at the scenery and living off the land whenever we

164

got the chance. The tenner only kept us going for about a week. We spent our last quid on petrol in New Plymouth and shot through to Rotorua, where I knew I could touch an old mate of mine for a couple of quid. We got there all right but young Jack was giving me a spell on the driving and he turned into my mate's driveway too fast for the brakes. We backed out of the wreckage of his gate and headed for Taupo.

"I got a job felling timber for a joker called Dan Hartshorne. A great big bloke he was. Stood a good twenty-four hands. About four axe-handles across the shoulders, face on him like a pine-cone and hard as a fencer's fingernail. He took us up to the job to give us a workout before lunch.

"Things were just going nicely. You could smell the tucker getting cooked down at the camp; and then young Jack has to go and put the lid on everything again. The boss was perched on the end of a log, watching me scarf a matai when Jack drops a tree fair across the other end of the log the boss was sitting on.

"What a performance! Scotty old boy, if I live to be a thousand I'll never see another dive like the one that bloke took into the gully when the end of that log sprung up on him. He lifted about thirty feet straight up in the air, hung there for a moment and then glided out over the creek. He hit a young horopito and it shot him across into a bunch of lawyer like a dirty great coil of winch-rope. He fell through that into the creek. It would have killed an ordinary bloke, Scotty, but Dan hardly had a scratch on him. I've heard the odd bit of swearing in me day but Dan's little effort when he came up out of that creek would have blistered these bricks. Jack and I didn't wait around to hear all of it, we took to our scrapers. Never even got a feed out of it. We had to sneak back after dark and milk a few gallons of diesel out of his tractor because we were just about out of gas.

"By this time the tucker situation was getting a bit desperate. We hadn't had a feed for three days. We headed for Taranaki and I had a look round in a shed at the back of someone's place in Wanganui to see if I could find some petrol. There was a full gallon tin sitting beside a motor mower so I took that. When we ran out of juice I grabbed the tin to pour in the tank and spilt a bit. It was varnish.

"When it got daylight I walked along to the nearest farm and sold the tin of varnish to the cocky for twenty quid. Told him I was with the Marine Department and the varnish was a special kind of fish-oil to prevent rickets in lambs. He lapped it up.

"Jack had gone the other way looking for some petrol. He'd knocked up an old girl and just about had her talked into parting with a couple of gallons when he stood on the cat and got booted off the place. She must have been one of those cat-loving types. We had to wait till nearly midday for a lift into town. And here's me expecting the bloke who bought the varnish to come bowling along any minute. It was after dark by the time we got away from there.

"If only that tree hadn't fallen back on my mate we wouldn't have had all that trouble."

Scotty spat on the ground. "You can't really blame the young feller for that, Sammy," he said.

"No, I don't s'pose so, Scott. But I got really saddled with him in the finish. Couldn't move but what Jack was hanging round watching everything a man did. Like a young dog or something. And we weren't getting anywhere — neither of us."

"What'd y' do, Sam? Shoot through on 'im?"

"Well, you could call it that, Scott. Y'see, we got a job working for an old tart who had a bit of a sheep- and cattle-run in the Hawke's Bay and it was such a good lurk it looked like getting permanent on us. I'd tried to get young Jack interested in a little place of his own but I could see he wasn't going to have it on unless I came too. And I wasn't having that on at any price. If a man wanted to latch on to kids he'd a got a job school-teaching. I couldn't even go on the bash when we were cashed-up because me mate wasn't the sort of bloke a man likes to lead astray. So in the end I decided the only way out of it was to do a moonlight on him.

"It took nearly a week to get a chance to sneak down on my own and see the old girl we were working for. Told her I was gettin' keen on her and had to shove off because I couldn't trust myself not to do something bad. That rocked her, I can tell you. I thought it'd get me kicked off the place quicker than spending a quid; but she ups and tells me to give her a few days to think about it. So I said I'd go away for four days and then come back if I still felt the same. I told her Jack was going to stay on and help with the work.

"Then I went up and told Jack the old girl had been making improper suggestions to me and I had to beat it out of there. I said she'd asked if he could stay and help out till she got someone else.

"The young bloke just about broke down on me. He wanted me to stay the night and go next morning but I couldn't risk it. I bet there was hell to pay when they told each other why I left."

"Bit rough, walking out like that, Sam"

"Hell, Scott! A man's got to keep moving."

"But be blowed. Besides, look at the spot you'd be in if I hadn't turned up here — no free smokes, no uplifting conversation, no true life experiences of Sam Cash to brighten your misery."

Scotty pinched out his cigarette and put the butt in his pocket.

"You're a queer one, Sam," he said. "You should have been a lawyer or something."

"I was," said Sam.

"What, a lawyer?"

"No, something — here comes our pet screw to take us on another little conducted tour."

"Righto, line up, you men!" called the warder. "Form two files — come along there, Cash, MacLean. We haven't got all day. You've had ten minutes extra out here as it is. Come on, MacLean."

"Hang on a minute there, mate!" said Sam. "Give the old bloke a chance. The trouble with you blokes is. . ."

"Quiet!"

And Sam was quiet.

NINE BOB AN HOUR

One last cloud lay across the sky like a rotten hunk of wood falling slowly to pieces. The yard below the house looked like an old battlefield with its scattered hulks of old truck-cabs and chassis standing untidily about. Sheep on the hills beyond were already grazing their way towards shade and water. It was going to be a stinking hot day.

Someone moved in another room. Sam smoothed over a couple of folds in the roughly-made bed and climbed quietly out the window, lifting his suitcase out after him. He circled the house at a respectable distance in case of dogs, then went up the path and knocked loudly on the back door. Sure enough, a mangy old cattle-dog ran belatedly out from under the tool shed, growled once, woofed twice, sniffed Sam's trouser-leg and waved his tail in reserved approval.

The door opened and an untidy kid looked shyly out.

"Your father up yet?" asked Sam.

"He's still in bed," announced the four-year-old boy.

"Well nick in and tell the lazy hound that Sam Cash wants to see him, will you."

The young fellow ducked out of sight and ran through the house calling "Daddy, the lazy hound wants to see you!"

Sam grinned and put his case on the porch. There were voices and sounds and a big man in pyjamas and overcoat came to the door.

"Sam Cash, you old sod! Come on in! When did you hit town? I heard you were up north with Goldson's Transport."

"Just arrived," said Sam blandly. "I got your telegram okay but one or two things held me up."

"Telegram?" said Joe puzzled. "Oh, I remember. But that was over eighteen months ago! We finished that contract just before last Christmas."

"Yeah," agreed Sam. "As I said, I got a bit side-tracked. How's tricks anyway, Joe? Still on the logs?"

"Yeah. I've got four logging units on the road at present. And if I get another contract I've put in for I'll be buying a new outfit for it — I'll need a good driver, if you're interested."

"Hell," said Sam disgustedly, "I wish I'd known, Joe. They've just about got me talked into taking over a mill up Pohukawa way. Twelve bob an hour. I've practically accepted it — er — what are you paying just now, Joe?"

"Well most of my chaps get eight bob or eight and six and they work their own hours. A good man can knock out his twenty-five notes a week."

"Hm." Sam looked thoughtful. Then: "Tell you what I'll do with you, Joe. Make it nine bob an hour and I'll try and put this mill crowd off. It won't be easy but I think I can swing it. You gave me a fair spin on that bulk-lime contract and I wouldn't like to see you put a crook driver on a new truck."

"I don't know whether I can afford nine bob," said Joe. "It's pretty big dough."

"You can't afford not to pay good money, the way things are in the logging business," corrected Sam. "You need a man who knows timber from felling to classing, in this caper. Half the blokes on trucks these days don't know one end of a spanner from the other. I've seen contractors go broke through drivers who put their trucks in the garage every time they get a loose battery-terminal or a spark-plug lead comes off."

"You've got something there," admitted Joe. "Anyway you'd better stay and have a bit of breakfast with us and we'll talk it over. I should hear about this other contract today or tomorrow. Where are you staying, by the way? There's a spare room out back you're welcome to use till we get you settled into a hut out at the job."

"That's pretty decent of you, Joe," said Sam, "but are you sure I won't be in the way?"

"No, there's tons of room here. The spare room hasn't been used for weeks."

Sam and Joe were inspecting the new diesel logging unit.

"She'll set me back a fair bit but she's a nice outfit," said Joe.

"Yeah," said Sam bending over a rear wheel. "Pay for itself in no time," said Joe.

"Yeah," said Sam looking underneath.

"She should take a good six or seven thousand feet," said Joe.

"Yeah," said Sam from under the bonnet.

"Get years of work out of her if she's looked after," said Joe.

"Yeah," said Sam examining the front suspension.

"Well, I'll go and tell them we'll take her," said Joe.

"No," said Sam straightening up.

"What?"

"Don't rush into anything, Joseph old boy," said Sam rolling a smoke. "We'll save ourselves a few bob here."

"How's that?"

"Just let me handle it," said Sam leading the way towards the office.

"Yes, gentlemen," said the manager. "What can I do for you?"

"We're interested in the logging unit," Sam informed him.

"Yes, sir. Hire-purchase or cash?"

"Cash," said Sam. "But we don't want to buy the whole thing at once. We'll buy the chassis, the cab and the motor and gearbox off you today. Tomorrow we'll buy the wheels, tyres, cab, trailer and all the other bits and pieces like seats, windscreen, doors and things."

The manager looked bleakly at Sam as though he'd just suggested something indecent and Joe asked "What's the idea of all that?"

"It just means that you buy a truck today, which isn't a deductible expense on your tax. Tomorrow you buy accessories and parts for a truck, which are deductible. You save yourself about fifty quid in tax and get the parts ten per cent cheaper than if you buy the works outright."

The manager didn't seem to like this idea at all.

"You realise, sir," he said sarcastically, "that this is a most unusual way of doing business."

"Perfectly legal," said Sam. "You don't blame a man for saving a few bob, do you? It's just good business."

"You realise that we could take all the parts off the vehicle and replace them at your expense."

"Yeah, you could," agreed Sam with a grin, "but it wouldn't be worth it, would it?"

"One thing," said the manager resignedly. "May I ask where you got this idea from?"

"Yeah," said Sam helpfully. "Out of a bully-beef tin."

And that's how Sam Cash came to be driving a new logging truck for Joe Halstead, for nine bob an hour.

NINE AND SIX AN HOUR

Joe dragged his utility to a savage stop outside the depot with a shower of gravel and a grim look on his face.

"Has anyone seen Sam Cash?" he asked the small group of men who were standing around the trucks.

"Not since the day before yesterday," said a short, fat, red-haired bloke wearing a black singlet and a G.M.C. truck.

"Where was he?"

"In his truck, going like a bat out of hell, heading towards Mokau."

"He's not at Mokau," said the beady-eyed little yardman. "Cliff and I came up from there last night."

"Then where in hell is he?" roared Joe.

But nobody knew.

"He's got to be found. They're damn near frantic up at the bush. They've got so much timber piled up at the skids that they can't cut another log. There's eight men up there doing their blocks, they're all on contract. Steve, you take the Chev and head over to Tirau and find out if anyone over that way has seen Sam's truck. Bung, you take the pick-up and have a look round Wairakei. You might as well go on to Taupo and see if you can pick up any news of him there. Cliff, you can nick across to Mangakino and have a look there.

"I've rung the police and there's no accidents reported but keep an eye open in case he's run off the road somewhere. And if you find him tell him to get back here with that truck or I'll put the cops on to him!"

The three vehicles roared out of the yard and Joe paced, impatiently around worrying about his new truck and working out a few suitable fates for Sam.

Bung found him. Late that afternoon in a pub not far from Taupo, drinking and yarning with a couple of bushmen as though he hadn't a care in the world, which was the case. There was no

177

sign of the new truck. "You're in for it this time, Sam. Joe's really raving!"

"Good," said Sam. "Have a beer."

"No, I'd better not. I've got to get back to the depot. Joe's waiting there. Where's your truck?"

"I sold it," said Sam.

"Strike, Sam! Joe'll murder you. He said if you don't get the truck back straight away he'll get the cops on to you."

"Listen, Bungy boy," said Sam. "When *you* start paying my wages I'll start taking orders from you. Go back and tell Joe that if he wants me to do anything he can come and see me about it. I'll be here for a couple of days yet. Now if you're not going to shout us a beer you'd better get crackin'. You're interrupting a good yarn."

"But the bush-boss is going mad! All his men are idle. There's so many logs piled up there that they can't work!"

"Yeah, that's right," said Sam. "By the way, when you see Joe tell him to bring a few quid with him, will you? I'm running a bit low."

Joe's utility broadsided to a stop outside the pub late that night and Joe trod into the bar with a look of black fury on his face and a clenched fist in each trouser-pocket. Sam turned as he approached.

"G'day, Joe," he said as though the meeting was entirely unexpected. "You going to shout? — a fresh beer, thanks barman."

"Where's the truck?" grated Joe.

"I've got 'er hidden in the scrub up the road a bit," Sam lowered his voice confidentially. "You never want to park your truck outside the pub when you're having a day or two on the grog, Joe," he warned. "It gives the firm a bad name. Besides that, the cops get to take too much notice of you — you're just in time to shout."

Joe was still glaring stonily, keeping himself under control almost by sheer physical strength.

"Is the truck all right?"

"Yeah, good as gold. Here, drink this. You're holding up the round." Sam shoved a drink into Joe's hand.

"Why aren't you up at the job? There's eight men sitting on

178

their backsides up there. Arthur Drew's been on the phone every hour for the last two days. You're lucky I didn't get the cops on to you!"

"Just as well you didn't," said Sam. "You'd have looked as silly as old Arthur is."

"I'll be damn lucky if I don't lose the contract over this," said Joe belligerently. "What's the idea, anyway?"

"The idea," said Sam, "is the only sensible one. Who's in charge of that outfit up there, anyway? Arthur Drew is just an independent contractor, same as the rest of us. Have you been down to the mill lately?"

"No, I've been too busy chasing you up."

"They've got enough logs piled up on the mill skids to keep them going for a fortnight," announced Sam. "If I dump any more there they won't be able to reach them with their winch rope, and you know what that means — double handling, at your expense. Our contract is to put the logs on the mill skids. I'm not making two dumps of it just to please old Arthur. You'd be broke inside a month. I had a natter with the mill manager about it and we decided that the best thing was for me to take it easy for a few days. Give them a chance to clear up round the place."

"Why the hell wasn't I told about it?" asked Joe, who was beginning to subside a little.

"Joe," said Sam, passing him a fresh glass of beer, "if you couldn't trust me to handle a thing like that without pestering you about it I wouldn't be earning my pay — incidentally, you couldn't lend me a fiver, could you?"

"No, I bloody well couldn't," said Joe. "There's a small matter of a bill for one Bedford motor that came in. Where did that come from?"

"Oh that," said Sam. "I told them to send that in. The motor in Pete's Beddy ground an oval crankshaft on herself so I lent him my truck for the day and slapped a new motor in for him. The old one was pretty dicey on it. Pays us to replace that old gear."

"Who told you to do that?" demanded Joe.

"Common sense, Joe. Common sense. They were waiting for a load of chain over in Napier and Pete didn't want to hold them up."

179

"What did you do with the old motor?" asked Joe.

"I gave it away," said Sam nonchalantly.

"You what?"

"I gave it to the bloke for the use of his shed and gear to switch the motors," said Sam. "It was a shrewd move too. That way we got the truck back on the road without losing a day. They don't like to be kept waiting on that Napier run. You can lose a lot of business that way."

Joe was almost smiling.

"Okay, okay. When do you think you can get back on the job?"

"Oh a couple of days will be plenty of time," said Sam carelessly.

"There's no doubt about you, Sam," said Joe with a slight grin as he reached over to put some money on the bar. "I'd have given another man the bullet, but — I don't know."

"Oh you couldn't afford to sack me," said Sam airily. "I save you too much money. And talking of money, I'll have to ask you for a raise."

"You what?" roared Joe.

"I'll have to touch you for a raise," repeated Sam. "With having to go steady on this contract I'm not clocking up enough hours to make decent wages. That's why I'm reduced to having to borrow that fiver off you. You see, Joe . . ."

And that's how Sam Cash came to be driving Joe Halstead's logging truck for nine and six an hour.

YOU NEVER KNOW

Joe and Cliff pulled up in Joe's utility at Sam's hut one lunchtime on their way to pick up a new timing-chain for Cliff's truck.

"Look, Sam," said Joe. "Things have been going pretty smoothly down here lately. There's not much point in me coming down just to check the tallies and pay the men. How about taking over this end of things altogether for me, so I can put in more time on the general carting?"

"No thanks, Joe," said Sam. "I'm signed on here as a truck driver, not a pen-pusher."

"But there's only about half an hour's book-work a day," protested Joe. "You could handle it easy."

"I could handle it all right," said Sam. "But I don't believe in making a boss out of myself. There's been blokes on this job for two years and I've only just started. It wouldn't be right for me to start slinging orders and pay-packets around. I've got to work with these blokes, you know."

"But you're the only one I could rely on not to make a botch of it," said Joe. "Cliff here handles the top end without any trouble."

"No offence, Joe," said Sam, "but I'm not the man for the job. It's too permanent for me anyway. And besides, I haven't touched a foreman's job since I saw what it did to poor old Harvey Wilson."

"Who was he, Sam?"

"Just a mate of mine. We used to hang around together a fair bit. No education, old Harvey, but when it came to nutting out a problem he could show a lot of these university blokes a thing or two. Too many brains, if you ask me. That's how he got himself into trouble, but it was through tackling a foreman's job that it all started in the first place."

"How was that?" asked Joe, interested.

"Well, it was like this," said Sam, getting out his tobacco. "Harvey and I paid off a coastal boat and lost every cracker we

183

had in a pakapoo den in Greys Avenue. You couldn't get a job round Auckland at the time if you offered to work for nothing, so we hopped a train and wound up on the bones of our backsides in Putaruru a day or two later.

"Things were tough there too. The only job even Harvey could jack up for us was cutting and peeling pine posts on a block thirty mile out. We had to have a go at it but I took one look at the place and wanted us to give it away and lean on our luck. About half a dozen pairs of blokes were dragging short ends and branches out of the tangles and mud on a broken-up block of worked-over pine and cutting posts out of them. All bow-saw work, too. No chainsaws in them days. Then the bark had to be peeled off them with a hand knife and the finished article was man-handled out through the mud and branches and stacked by the track. All this for the handsome sum of thirty bob a hundred. One poor coot had just fished out a broken end the tractor had ground into the mud. After he got it out where he could work on it he scraped all the mud off it and found out it was shattered all to hell. So he dived back into the mess like a dog in a rabbit hole to look for another hunk.

"I tell you Joe. She was the most gruesome-looking caper I've ever clapped me lookin' gear on!

"To hell with this, I says to Harvey. We'd never make our tucker in this dump.

"But Harvey just stood there looking round as though he'd lost something. Then: Sammy, he says to me, I reckon we can make our stake here. Let's go and see the boss."

"So you took it on, eh?" said Joe. "Did you do any good at it?"

"Joe," said Sam, kicking a stone against the wheel of his truck, "I knew Harvey Wilson for close on fifteen years and I never once heard of him taking on anything he didn't do good at. We did better on those posts than anyone had ever done before."

"You must have put in some work on it," said Cliff.

"No fear," said Sam. "We did less work than any of the other teams and put out twice as many posts. We sailed straight in and knocked out five hundred posts in the first week. But they still had to be trimmed, and that was the hardest part. Then Harvey borrows an old H.D.-five and ploughs it back and forth over our big heap of posts. In a couple of hours he had most of the bark bruised off them. All we had to do was knock off the bits he'd missed with the axe and stack them up.

"We drew six or seven quid that week and the other blokes there were lucky to knock out their thirty bob or two quid.

"By the end of a month Harvey and I had a big rumbler rigged up on the job and all we did was rumble the bark off the other blokes' posts for ten bob a hundred. We cleaned up a nice comfortable roll each in no time and I wanted to call it quits and shoot through, but Harvey was a bit hard to head off once he got his hooks into something no one else had ever done. He talked the boss into putting in our own creosote tanks and we all treated all our own posts. Then they opened up another block and slapped Harvey in charge of it.

"He designed a new kind of peeler and as far as I know they're using the same type of thing today. Then he worked out an improved treatment process and it wasn't long before the Government got to hear about him and offered him a job in charge of a big new timber-treatment plant they were starting at Milton Downs.

"This was a bit too much for me and I tried to talk Harvey out of getting himself mixed up in it but he had the bit between his teeth good and proper by this time. Nothing I said made any difference. He took it on and I had to split up with him.

"Next thing I hear is that Harvey is in full charge of fifteen hundred men and about half a million quid's worth of equipment. But I knew it was going to blow up on 'im. You could see it coming as plain as next weekend."

"How could it blow up on him if he was such a bright bloke?" asked Cliff.

"He was too good for his own good," replied Sam. "Harvey no sooner got everything organised than all the bums and no-hopers he'd ever bludged a beer off or worked with turned up wanting soft jobs. I knew some of them and a bigger bunch of ratbags you never saw in all your born days. But Harvey had pretty strong ideas about helping his mates out and every man jack of them got a nice cushy job and a week's pay in advance.

"There was Bludger Bill Jenkins, from Taihape, who'd never

swung an axe in his life, in charge of one of the bush gangs. Double-Header Danny from Wellington, who'd never been further inland than the Pier Hotel, secured the position of Personnel Officer on the strength of him having lent Harvey a couple of quid once. And Big Aussie Newcombe came over from Sydney to handle the sly-grog end of things, with Harvey cut in on a third of the profits. Freddy the Burglar was selected as Chief Fire Officer. They gave him a new Land Rover and he took off for Tauranga to pick up a couple of his cobbers and it was three months before they got their wagon back. They never heard from Freddy again till the next Supreme Court Sessions. — I tell you, Joe, by the time Harvey handed in his resignation he was the only honest bloke left on the job."

"Hell, Sam," said Joe. "I'll bet he was in trouble over that lot!"

"Trouble?" said Sam. "I'll say he was in trouble. It took the Clerk of the Court three-quarters of an hour to read out the charges against him at the depositions. Then they had to ask for an indefinite adjournment so they could get all the evidence sorted out.

"If they ever get those fifteen hundred witnesses and all the exhibits and files and records and Harvey Wilson in the same place at the same time, they'll probably sue him for his back teeth. But I wouldn't like their job. Harvey's been running around on five hundred quid bail for the last ten years and they still haven't sorted it all out."

"But that's not likely to happen here," laughed Joe, returning to the original purpose of the interview.

"You can say that again," said Sam. "I'm sorry, Joe, but I can't tackle it. No matter how good some blokes are at a job they're just not the right types to put in charge of other blokes. And I'm one of them.

"Now if you blokes haven't got anything better to do than stand round here gossiping all afternoon, I have. Got to get another four loads of logs down to the skids before they knock off."

As Joe and Cliff drove away, Cliff said: "Sam's a beaut, isn't he! What a fantastic line of bull! He doesn't expect us to believe all that does he?"

"You never know with Sam," said Joe. "I've known him for a good few years, on and off, and I'd be the last to call him a liar."

"But what about all that business of his mate mucking up a big Government project?" asked Cliff incredulously.

"You just can't be sure," insisted Joe. "I remember once Sam told a few of us a yarn about him being called in to advise the Minister of Defence about defending the East Coast in case of invasion during the war. One of the blokes, a big Irishman called Paddy O'Shea, got up and called Sam a fake and a phoney and threatened to knock his block off for expecting him to swallow such a pack of lies."

"What did Sam do?" asked Cliff.

"He just walked out of the hut without a word," said Joe. "We thought he must have been a bit yellow, especially when he didn't turn up for work next day."

"I can't imagine Sam backing out of anything, even if he is a bit of a bull-artist," said Cliff, disappointed.

"Bull-artist be blowed," said Joe. "And he didn't back out of anything. He turned up at the job at lunchtime a couple of days later and handed Paddy a sealed letter from the ex-Minister of Defence in Wellington, saying that he was deeply indebted to Sam Cash for his invaluable advice and assistance in his defence programme during the last war. On special paper, it was, with a flash letterhead and signed all legal. There was no doubt it was genuine all right. It seems Sam used to run a little fishing boat up and down the coast and poked into all the little creeks and bays. He knew the coast like the back of his hand and all the country for miles inland. Where all the fresh water was, and everything.

"He passed the letter round for all of us to read and then gave Paddy the biggest thrashing I've ever seen a man handed for calling him a liar. They ended up the best of mates after that, but I'd be very careful about calling Sam Cash a liar, if I were you. You just never know."

A SHREWD MOVE

"I don't know, Sam, said Joe. "You've got me beat! If you wanted to settle down and put your mind to it you could make a real success of yourself at just about anything you liked. But just when you look like coming right you turn round and get yourself into some sort of trouble."

"You could call me a successful failure," grinned Sam.

Joe wasn't amused. "This business of burning down old Snotty's hut, now. It might have been an accident in the first place but some of the boys are saying you just stood there and didn't even give the old bloke a hand to save a bit of his gear. It's not like you not to help a mate in trouble, Sam — that's probably how the rumour started that you set fire to his hut in the first place."

"Yeah," said Sam. "I did."

"Do you mean to say you deliberately set fire to old Snotty's hut and then stood there and let everything he owned go up in smoke?" Joe was incredulous.

"Yeah, sure," said Sam. "It was a shrewd move that."

"A shrewd move, was it?" said Joe grimly. "Well old Snotty's pretty popular round here and a lot of people have been asking me what I'm going to do about it."

"That a fact?"

"If that's all you've got to say about it, Sam," said Joe in resignation, "I'll have to put you off. I hate to have to do it, but pulling a dirty trick like that on an old bloke doesn't let you in for any consideration. I must say I'm pretty disappointed in you, Sam."

"Righto," said Sam carelessly. "I'll pick up my cheque this afternoon. It's time I was shoving off anyway."

Joe opened the door of his utility and paused with one foot inside.

"I can't make you out at all," he hesitated. "What did poor old Snotty ever do to you?"

"Answer me this one," said Sam leaning on the mudguard and fishing out his tobacco. "How old do you reckon Snotty is?"

"Going on seventy, isn't he?"

"Yeah. And how long has he been living in that old hut down by the swamp?"

"Must be a good few years," said Joe thoughtfully. "He came here just after the war."

"Fifteen years he lived in that hut," agreed Sam. "And they've never spent a penny on it the whole time. They've had him working on that muddy bloody track they call a road for six rotten quid a week because the old bloke's too proud to put in for a pension. They couldn't get another man to take that job on for less than twenty quid a week and they're too mean and miserable to shift him into a dry hut.

"I'll tell you why I burnt Snotty's hut down, Joe. Because he wouldn't have seen another winter out in that stinking bog hole. I wouldn't tie a dog up in the blasted place!

"I went down there the other day with a cabbage for the old boy and there he is trying to block out the wind with old bits of sack. Blankets so wet and mouldy you could hardly lift them. He had to wring out his strides before he put them on and half an inch of mould and mildew over everything. Rats running everywhere and the only firewood he had was what I used to drop off for him on my way home, after I'd seen him dragging pine branches from half a mile down the road!"

"Look, Sam. I didn't know it was that bad," said Joe frowning.

"It wasn't that bad at all, Joseph old boy. It was a blasted sight worse! And you come and tell me old Snotty's popular round here. Nobody seemed to notice how popular he was till he lost what little he owned."

"Still," interrupted Joe, "that's no excuse to burn other people's property."

"Excuse!" cried Sam. "What sort of an excuse does a man need? And where's old Snotty right now? He's up in that old house of Blakely's that's been empty for five years! With a proper stove and plenty of firewood! Right handy to his job. With more warm blankets and clothes than he knows what to do with. There's been stuff arriving for Snotty from all over the place. He even got a good push-bike off Jack Brewster, who's watched Snotty carry his gear on his back for years since somebody ran over his bike with a truck. And a cheque came yesterday for him from some society or other in Auckland. If Snotty lives to wear out all the gear he's been given since he got burnt out he'll be with us for a long time yet.

"Oh yes. He's popular all right," concluded Sam. "So popular a man has to burn his hut down so he won't die in a swamp among the rats!"

Joe was dismayed. "But Sam," he spluttered. "Snotty never said anything to anyone about his hut. We thought he was happy enough down there!"

"Snotty's not a moaner," said Sam. He thought a moment. "It's got that way there's so many moaners around that a bloke who's too proud to grovel and whine just gets forgotten and left to die like a dog."

Sam moved away shaking his head.

"Where are you going?" asked Joe.

"I've got a bit of gear to sort out," replied Sam. "I'll bring the truck up and leave it in the yard when I pick up my cheque."

"Look, Sam," said Joe. "How about forgetting it? I didn't know you were only helping old Snotty out. I . . . I'd like you to stay on."

"No thanks, Joe," said Sam. "It's time I shoved off. No hard feelings, but I've been here over two months and I like to clock up a bit of mileage now and then. It keeps a man's wheel bearings from seizing up."

"Well, you're going to be a hard man to replace," said Joe, realising that nothing he said would change Sam's mind. "If you want to come back any time there'll be an empty truck here for you whenever you want it . . . nine and six a hour," he added with a grin.

As Joe shook Sam's hand outside his office he said "I don't think they'll take any action about you burning that hut down, Sam, but if they do I'll pay them for the damage."

"No fear," said Sam. "Don't pay them a cracker. Nothing'd suit me better than to get up in public and tell the whole damn world how they treated old Snotty. And he's just one of thousands.

"We call ourselves civilised, Joe, but you'd never get a Maori or an Abo or an islander to treat his old folk the way we do. We send thousands of quid to hard-up people in other countries but half our own grandfathers are waiting around in the pubs to die because they had the cheek to grow old and nobody reckons old age is worth allowing for. Drunks they call 'em — and drunks they are. Wouldn't you be?

"Ah, here's Cliff with that load of pipes for the railhead. I'll get a lift in with him. See you round, Joe!"

Joe stood in the doorway and watched Sam throw his gear on the truck and climb into the cab.

"You ought to be shot or crowned, Sam," he muttered. "But I don't know which."

OLD HAMMERGUN

The weather couldn't make up its mind whether it was on Sam's side or not and he was undecided whether to carry on to Waitu or stay at the pub where the last ride he'd hitched had brought him.

The steady stream of traffic along the road eventually persuaded him he could pick up a lift through to Waitu easy enough, so he swung off down the road, thumbing the cars as they went past.

Two hours later rain was obviously a lot closer than the lift he'd hoped for and it was beginning to grow dark. He was well into the narrow Rakitura Gorge where the road narrows and twists back and forth above the river, with bush growing thickly on either side. And there wasn't a house or even a hut for miles. The stream of cars had thinned to a few odd late ones hurrying past and none of them were going to stop and pick up a lone man in this part of the country at night.

Something would have to be done about it, if he was going to avoid spending a wet night on the roadside.

If they weren't going to stop and give a man a lift of their own accord they'd have to be made to. So at the next suitable place he came to Sam climbed the steep bank above the road and kicked and levered at a big rock that hung there till it crashed on to the road, bringing a shower of stones and clay with it. No matter which way the next car was going he would get a lift to the nearest pub and continue his journey the next day.

He was in luck. Within a few minutes a car travelling in his direction slowed and stopped, with Sam and his big rock lit up in the headlights.

"Hello, what's this?" said the lone occupant of the car, a middle-aged man as nondescript as his car, except that the whole outfit stank to Sam of too much money.

"Bit of a slip," he explained. "If we can just shift this rock out of the way we should be able to sneak past."

It was hardly more than a one-man job to roll the rock away and within a few minutes Sam had his lift to Waitu.

"You'll have to sit in the front," explained the man, wiping clay off his hands on a spotless handkerchief. "I've got my shotgun on the back seat. It's worth over two hundred quid and I don't want it bouncing around on the floor. Had it custom-made," he added with obvious pride.

Sam glanced into the car and saw the polished guncase lying across the back seat.

"So you do a bit of shooting?" said Sam, getting in beside the driver.

"Just a bit. That's my trap-gun. I've got another one I use for ducks and pheasant. I'm going down for the big shoot at Huntsville — do you do any shooting yourself?"

"I used to do a bit," admitted Sam, "but the price of the cartridges got a bit steep for me in the finish and I had to turn it in."

"It's a great sport," said the driver. "I wouldn't miss my trap-shooting for worlds."

"Yes, it's a fair enough caper," said Sam, "but it's the sort of thing a man's got to keep at all the time or he gets out of practice."

"Oh yes. You must practise," agreed the driver. "But a good gun is the most important thing."

"Wouldn't say that," said Sam. "The best shotgun-shot I ever knew used an old hammergun with Damascus-twist barrels that turned up about the same time as Captain Cook. Old Hammergun, we called him. He was a rabbiter up in the Hawke's Bay. Used to load his own cartridges and hung round the gun club when we were holding a shoot to collect all the empty shells.

"Nobody used to take much notice of Old Hammergun until the day I invited him to have a few shots with us. He'd never shot at clay-birds in his life but the old boy opened our eyes, I can tell you."

"Good shot eh?" chuckled the driver.

"It was a while before we could find out whether he was hitting them or not," said Sam. "Y'see, he broke out his own gun and cartridges and when he fired there was such a cloud of smoke and paper wadding we couldn't see what the hell was going on. He was loading 'em with blasting powder and they had to wait for the smoke to clear so they could release the next target.

"Then I lent him my gun and a handful of good shells and Old Hammergun turned on the best performance any of us had ever seen. We gave him every cartridge we had with us and sent one of the blokes for another couple of packets. We threw clays in every direction except straight at him and not one of them got more than a few feet from the trap-house before he blew it to bits. And when he handed me back my gun he told me it was all out of balance and wanted a couple of inches hacked off the end of the barrels.

"We put up a fiver for anyone who could stand on the tracks beside Old Hammergun and shoot a clay before he did. After a couple of weeks we raised it to fifty quid, and then seventy-five."

"Did anyone take the money?" asked the driver.

"Not on your life," said Sam. "They came for miles to have a go at that seventy-five quid. Experts with guns of every make, style, and description. Full choke to cylinder barrels of every length you could fire a cartridge out of. They handicapped Hammergun till he was so far back you'd swear he was out of range but with my old gun and number-four shot he didn't give them a chance. They offered him big money to represent a club up north in one of the international shoots but Hammergun wouldn't have it on. He just went on with his rabbiting, same as ever.

"We gave him the seventy-five quid to buy a new gun in the finish but he spent it on the grog. Reckoned his old hammergun would see him out. And it did. A couple of years later we all turned up at the cemetery and gave Old Hammergun a few good volleys as a send-off.

"We got hold of his old gun to put on the gun club wall with a little notice about Old Hammergun to remind the members that the first requirement in shooting is good judgment, and not to blame the gun when you miss. It's dead right too, the best gun in the world won't make a good shot out of a man with crook judgment."

"I suppose you're right," conceded the driver. "But good equipment is essential . . ."

"Good equipment," interrupted Sam, "takes more fun out of

life than hangovers. Catching a big fish on a heavy line and a flash rod isn't half the fun you get out of playing and landing him on light gear. Shooting a deer or pig with a high-powered rifle, with telescopic sights and special expanding ammunition is no trouble, but the man who can sneak up and hit them in the right place with an old Lee-Enfield with open sights and a barrel like a crank-handle — he's really done something. There's just not the same feeling of achievement when the odds are all on your side. Arriving somewhere in an old bomb that has had to be practically re-built along the way really gives a man the feeling that he deserves to have got there. But there's no achievement in floating along in a flash car that just about drives itself. The same applies to just about everything, once you think about it."

Lights from a building showed on the roadside up ahead.

"Here's Waitu," said Sam. "Just drop me off at the pub, will you, mate. It was good of you to stop and pick me up. Thanks a lot."

The driver pulled up outside the hotel to let Sam off and floated off in his flash car, with his custom-made shotgun on the back seat and something to think about.

NOTHING BUT THE BEST

Sam stopped by the white gate and looked across the farm. Fences all new and tight, the top of each post and batten painted with tar against rot and unsightliness. The row of pines behind the freshly painted house had been neatly and regularly topped and trimmed. Buildings neatly laid out and maintained. A house-cow in a clean new cover grazed in the kind of pasture you only get in return for annual applications of superphosphate at something like three cwt. to the acre. A chaff-fed pony walked curiously along the road fence towards him. The drive was evenly gravelled with a row of white painted stones along either side. A small creek wound through the farm with cool willow growing thickly along its banks. The paddock on his left was running about six well-bred Romneys to the acre and the one on the other side of the drive was sprouting a very promising crop of well-cultivated turnips. The vegetable-garden by the house would have made the pictures on the seed-packets look like burnt-over gorse, and away beyond the silvery blades of a windmill a low range of rough hills provided a pleasant contrast. A very nice little place indeed!

Sam sauntered whistling up the long driveway and hunted round the buildings till he found the farmer (Jim Ryan, according to the name on the letterbox) tacking battens on a fence behind his woolshed.

"I see you've got a few days' work for a good man," said Sam without preamble.

"Sorry mate," said the farmer flatly. "Things are pretty quiet just now. I can handle everything that needs doing round the place."

"I'd have thought you needed a man pretty badly," said Sam, leaning on the fence and rolling a smoke. "There's a week's work between here and the front gate."

"*My* front gate?"

"Yeah."

"What needs doing down there?" The man was obviously surprised.

"Well for a start it wants a bit of a drain put in to dry out that muddy corner the sheep have churned up down by the road. Then the whole corner wants fencing off into a triangle and a few blue-gums planting in there for shelter. If you ever get a mob of sheep jammed into that sharp corner half of them'll smother on you. Then there's that water-trough out in the paddock."

"What's wrong with that?"

"It'll have to be shifted," said Sam easily. "The sheep have worn the ground around it so deep that they're having a job to reach the water. Most of them are drinking at the creek down the far end of the paddock. You'll never keep condition on sheep that have to travel that far for water in this type of country. The trough should never have been put there in the first place. We'll have to shift it right over by that clump of trees past the gate so your sheep won't have to leave the shade to get a drink. That hedge you've just planted along the drive will have to come out too."

"There's nothing wrong with that hedge," cried Jim Ryan, who prided himself that he had the best kept farm in the district, which was precisely why Sam had singled him out for attention.

"It's a damn good hedge," said Sam, "but it's on the wrong side of the fence. All your wind comes from the west here — look at the lean on those trees there. As soon as that hedge grows up enough to catch the wind it's going to get blown out into the paddock on an angle and you'll never get a decent growth. We'll have to shift it on to the west side of the fence so it'll get blown against it. By the time the fence falls to bits it'll be in the middle of a good solid hedge that way."

"This is the best kept place around here," said Jim Ryan defensively. He was distinctly taken aback by this long skinny character who'd come sloping up out of nowhere and started picking holes in the layout of his farm. "I don't need to be told how to . . ."

"Oh she'll be pretty good once we get a few rough edges knocked off her," Sam agreed. "Unfortunately I won't be able to spend more than a week or two with you, but we should get a fair bit straightened out if we get stuck into it. This is the time of year to do all these odd jobs, with nothing to do to the sheep till dipping — that dip of yours wants another few feet stuck on the end of it too, by the way. It's about four feet too short. A sheep wouldn't be in that thing long enough for the solution to soak through the fleece properly. You'd have the inspectors on your neck in no time."

Jim Ryan looked across at his flash new sheep-dip and then back at Sam.

"But that plan was recommended by the stock agent," he said indignantly. "It's the best dip around here!"

"It was probably designed for freshly-shorn sheep," explained Sam kindly. "We'll soon get her right for you though."

In the days that followed Sam heard nothing but how some part of Jim Ryan's farm or some bit of his gear was "the best around".

They fenced off the corner by the gate and planted trees in it.

"That's the best corner I've got now," said Jim proudly.

They shifted the hedge and the water-trough.

"The best laid-out paddock around!"

They knocked the end out of the dip and concreted another three-foot-six on to it.

"The best dip around!"

They tore down a dividing fence and created the best lambing-paddock around. Then they put up a dividing fence to make the best holding-paddock around. They took the wheels off the tractor and turned them round for greater width, making it the best hillside tractor around. They threw out an old tea-chest and two forty-four gallon drums and built the best three dog kennels for the three best dogs around.

The best housewife around got the best clothes-line and the best hay-sweep was put outside under the trees to make room in the best implement shed for the best concrete-mixer and the best wheelbarrow. The best footbridge got knocked to bits and the best culvert put in for access to the best fifty acres of steep and broken scrub and bush around.

After three weeks of this the best farmer around began to get on Sam's nerves a bit. Even at a fiver a day. He was saved taking action when Jim admitted one morning that he didn't have another thing that needed doing. Sam modestly pocketed a cheque for the best wages Jim had ever paid a man and prepared to depart. They were saying goodbye by the hayshed and Jim was loudly claiming the best of everything for himself and his farm when Sam suddenly said: "Who put this hay in here?"

"I did," said Jim. "What's wrong with it? It's the best crop of hay we've had for years. Eighty bales to the acre, as a matter of fact."

"There's nothing wrong with it yet," said Sam, "but there will be if it's not lifted higher off the ground pretty soon. Once this stuff gets wet she generates heat, and it's damp already. Have a look for yourself. You'll have a fire in there within three months. I guarantee it. The whole lot will have to come out and the boards underneath built up at least six inches higher. You could use the poles from the willows along the creek when you cut them down."

"Cut down those willows?" cried Jim. "That happens to be the best growth of willow around!"

"That's just why they'll have to come out," said Sam. "If you leave them much longer the root systems are going to choke up the whole works with a thick mat and the water won't be able to get past. Before you know where you are you'll get flooding, and swamps'll form out into the paddocks on each side. I reckon you'd lose about five acres a year, once she got started. Whoever planted golden willow in a place like that wants his backside kicked."

"Hey, wait a minute," said Jim hotly. "My father planted them there to hold the banks."

"Well he ought to have known better," said Sam. "Black poplar is the only thing to plant in a place like that. Write to the Department of Agriculture about it, they'll tell you. But first of all get those willows out of it. It's not as big a job as it looks, really. Once you put the wheels on the tractor back the other way so it'll go through that narrow gateway down there, and tack higher sides on your trailer so it'll take a decent load of branches. Of course it'd be better to widen all your gateways but if you do that the lambing'll be on you by the time you get your windmill replaced by a decent electric pump."

"That windmill has supplied the house with water for twenty years," announced Jim. "It's staying where it damn well is!"

"Then you can please yourself whether you pull it down or

leave it till the mainshaft wears right through and falls down and blocks the bore. But I'd be inclined to replace it as soon as possible. I give it another two months of wear, at the very most. And you know what it means to be short of water in the middle of summer."

"I'll put a new shaft in it," said Jim.

"A brass shaft for a windmill that size is going to set you back twenty or thirty quid," said Sam, "and by the time you replace all the worn bearings and slap a new set of blades on her it's going to cost you more than a complete new outfit. And you'll have to get everything made up. They don't make windmills parts any more. If I was you I'd get the bulldozer to shove the whole box-'n'-dice into the gully and put a proper pump in."

"What bulldozer?" said Jim with renewed hostility.

"What's the use of us having put in a culvert to cross the creek unless you 'doze an access road to get your tractor into that corner of the farm?" asked Sam in surprise. "I thought that was what we spread the wheels of the tractor for! You'll have to put in a couple of gateways over there too. It's got to be done if you want to bring all that rough country into pasture next year."

"Can you see anything else wrong with the place, while you're about it?" said Jim sarcastically.

"Nothing else that needs urgent attention," admitted Sam, "but you'll be busy enough; what with breaking in a new heading dog and replacing the floor under the shearing plant."

"Heading dog!" exploded Jim. "I'll have you know that Biddy happens to be the best little heading bitch around!"

"She probably is Jim, but your other two dogs are straight huntaways, and I don't know if you've noticed, but by lambing time Biddy is gong to be so heavy in pup that you won't be able to work her. That big Alsatian from next door hasn't been hanging around here to admire your farming technique, you know.

"Well, that bus'll be coming past any time now. I'd better get down and catch him. So long, Jim! Don't let them work you too hard now."

And Sam sauntered whistling down the long driveway, leaving Jim Ryan wondering whether it was worth the trouble trying to maintain the best farm around after all.

A LINE OF BULL

The van rattled and its driver prattled along the road at a speed that was only just this side of dangerous for both of them. Sam sat looking out the window at the farms, trying not to listen to the ceaseless chatter of his driver, without much hope of success. He'd been picked up twenty miles back by this secondhand-clothing peddler, who was returning to Kakahu after having got rid of his load.

"Yes," he was saying for the severalth time, "it's lucky for you I happened along. There's not much traffic on this road during the week — that's Andy Mason's place on the left in here. He usually takes a few quid's worth off me. The place on the right isn't worth stopping at. Two old maids live there and they're as tight as they come. Run their stock on the roadside most of the winter. . . . Yes, I picked up a lot of good stuff at that last jumble sale. Bought up the whole sale before it opened for twenty quid. That's the only way to make a profit. Deal big! . . . There's a swag of Maoris living in that place on the hill over there but none of them have ever got any money. You've got to catch them soon after Family Benefit day to do any good out of them. . . . That's old Fred Pritchard's place. He's no good either. He's still wearing a pair of pants I sold him two years ago. He gets a new shirt off me every Christmas, but during the year it's not worth stopping there. Yes, you're lucky I picked you up all right!"

Sam's benefactor cut the van round a blind corner on the wrong side at thirty miles an hour and Sam's foot almost went through the floorboards.

"You'd have still been walking."

They passed a farm where a man was trying to get a bull into a crush in some yards near the road.

"There's Peter Atkins," gabbled the used-clothing merchant, waving dangerously out his window. "They're a fine couple that. They've got the biggest tribe of kids on my run. Always good for a few quid's worth and a cup of tea. But just between you and me I don't think they've been doing too well lately. There was no butter on the bread last time. Dripping!" The van slid madly round another blind corner.

"Yes, it's a good thing I happened along when I did," repeated the driver. "Must be your lucky day all right."

Sam had had enough.

"You can pull up and let me out here, thanks mate," he said.

"But I thought you were going to Ratapu Junction?"

"Changed me mind," said Sam climbing out and closing the door. "I don't want to push that luck of mine too far. Thanks for the lift."

Sam walked back to where the man, Peter Atkins, was still trying to get his bull into the crush and crossed to the yards.

"Like a hand, mate?"

"Hello! Where did you spring from?" asked the pleasant-faced young bloke who had been poking the bull through the rails with a long stick.

"I had a ride with your secondhand-clothes man," explained Sam. "But he got a bit too much for me. I saw you here and decided to stop and see if you wanted a hand. I'll pick up another lift later on when they get the wreckage of his van cleared away from one of those sharp bends!"

"Yes, old Powell's a bit of a talker isn't he," grinned the bloke. "But I don't think you've got much chance of picking up another ride on this road. It's very quiet along here."

"I'd swap the quiet for that bloke's ear-bashing any time," said Sam, "and I've got more chance of getting there in one piece if I don't have to be transferred into a coffin halfway . . . I'm Sam Cash, by the way. What do they call you when they can't catch you?"

"Plenty," said Pete. "But all the bills come to Pete Atkins. Pleased to meet you, Sam."

"Glad to know you, Pete," said Sam shaking hands with him. "What's the old boy here been up to?"

Pete poked the muddy Shorthorn bull in the ribs with his stick.

"I'm trying to get him into the crush so I can put a ring in his nose," he explained. "He's been knocking my fences around and

I thought a ring with a few feet of light chain through it might quieten him down a bit."

"That ought to do the trick," agreed Sam.

"He's not too keen on the idea of going into the crush," said Pete.

"Might be a better idea to rope him," said Sam. "He's liable to knock himself around a bit if you try to ring him in the crush. And you haven't got much room to work in there. If he catches your hand against the rails you can lose a lot of hide. Makes 'em yard-shy too."

"Have you done them before?" asked Peter.

"Yeah. One or two," said Sam modestly. "Have you got a couple of good strong ropes handy?"

"Won't take me a minute to go down and get them," said Pete. "That's if you don't mind . . ."

"No," said Sam. "Only too glad of the exercise."

Pete half ran down the hill to the house and sheds among some trees, where Sam could hear children shouting, and was soon back with two thick ropes.

"Here you are, Sam," he said. "What's the drill?"

"You just watch for the time being," said Sam shaking out one of the ropes. "This is really only a one-man job."

He dropped a noose over the bull's horns and snubbed the other end tight to a corner-post. The bull pulled back and bellowed but was unable to prevent Sam from looping the other rope neatly round its neck. He threw the rope over the bull's withers and made a half-hitch round him behind the front legs. Then he passed the rope around the flanks in another half-hitch and handed the end of it to Pete.

"Just pull on that, straight back behind him, Pete."

Pete pulled on the rope and the bull buckled at all his knees at once and rolled over helpless in the mud. Pete was so astonished he nearly let the rope go.

"What's happened?" he asked. "I've got hardly any weight on the rope at all!"

"It just paralyses them for a little while," explained Sam.

"Doesn't do them any harm. Now have you got that ring handy?"

Pete kicked the ring and chain and a small screwdriver through the rails to him and Sam undid the locking-screw, drove the ring deftly through the bull's nose, slipped the chain on to it and screwed it up again.

"You can let him up again now, Pete," he said taking the noose off the bull's horns. "Just let the rope go and he'll step out of it when he gets up. If I was you I'd leave him in the yard tonight. If you let him out while he's still a bit indignant he's liable to run around and make his nose bleed. It'll take him a day or two to get used to the weight of the chain."

Pete could hardly believe his eyes when the bull stood up unharmed and began to walk up and down the yard shaking his head, with the ring and chain neatly hanging from his nose.

"Where did you pick that one up?" he asked in amazement.

"Oh, an old German bloke and I used to round up wild cattle in the Mamaku and sell them to the farmers," said Sam rolling a smoke. "That's how we used to cut all the bulls. I reckon old Otto would be about the best man on wild cattle from here to the black stump. He taught me all I know about 'em. But Otto's forgotten more about cattle than I'll ever learn."

"He must have been marvellous," said Pete enthusiastically.

"Yes, he was all right, all right," said Sam. "I once saw Otto go in and kill a raving mad bull with an axe. A big old Jersey, it was. One day it was so quiet the farmer's kids could go and sit all over it out in the paddock, and the next it charged everything that came near.

"Smashed the fowl-run. Rooted up a big hedge. Tipped over a haystack and wandered back and forth through everyone's fences, charging everything that moved. It wasn't safe to go within a mile of it. It took them a week to get all the stock back on the right farms afterwards.

"They called in the police and they called in the army. About a hundred soldiers and a dozen big six-wheelers lined up to do battle with this bull but all they could do was give orders not to shoot because there were people holed up in their houses all around and there was a risk of someone copping a stray bullet. Then they got the idea of sending for us. We were camped about fifteen mile away at the time.

"When Otto and I pulled up in our little truck there were Bren-guns and rifles and sandbags and trucks lined up along half a mile of the road, with sergeant-majors bellowing at blokes all over the place. The bull was about five hundred yards away, tossing hay all over the paddock and bellowing nearly as loud as the army blokes. One of them came over yelling at us to clear out because it was a danger zone.

"We didn't take any notice of them and Otto got his good axe off the back of the truck and said to me, 'Stay here and see that these noisy idiots don't interfere, Sam. I'll just nick in and fix this bull up.'

"I can tell you, Pete, I was a bit worried myself. That bull was as crazy as a bomb-thrower and just as dangerous. But Otto was as calm as a hot Sunday afternoon. He went over and lifted the gate into the paddock off its hinges and walked out towards the bull with the gate hooked over one shoulder and the axe over the other."

"A gate?" cried Pete.

"Yes, an ordinary five-bar, ten-foot gate," said Sam. "Every one thought he'd gone as mad as the bull and I must say my faith in him wavered a bit when I saw what he was doing. There was such a shouting and waving for him to come back that the bull stopped his hay-tossing and looked round to see what all the commotion was in aid of. When it saw Otto coming with a dirty big gate it trotted out to meet him and everyone shut up yelling and got up on to the trucks out of the way. It was suddenly so quiet that you could almost hear the smoke puffing out of Otto's old pipe as he went on over the paddock.

"They reckon those cowboys in the old days used to get a bit worked up when a couple of their mates went out into the road to fight it out, Pete, but the tension with Otto and that bull closing in on each other would have made a procession of fighting cowboys look like a game of Ludo.

"When the bull was about ten yards away from Otto it stopped and dug its horns into the ground. Dirt and grass flew twenty feet into the air but it wasn't too sure about tackling Otto because he wouldn't take to his scrapers like everything else had. So Otto charged the bull.

"He went up and dropped the top rail of his gate over the bull's horns and stepped out of the road. The bull tried to charge him but its front feet got caught in the bottom rails and before it could tear itself free Otto was in and chopped it fair through the back of the neck with a couple of quick swipes.

"When the bull went down Otto wiped the blood off his axe-head on the carcass and checked the edge with his thumb. Then he came back across the paddock, still puffing on his old pipe.

"Suddenly all hell broke loose. A gang of soldiers sneaked up on the dead bull and pumped about fifty shots into it to make sure, and such a yelling and shouting you never heard in all your born days. But old Otto just pushed his way through the crowd and got into the truck with me. 'Gapped me axe, Sam,' he says to me. 'Let's get out of here before they start going crook about their gate.'

"And Otto never mentioned that bull again as long as I knew him."

"No wonder you're so good with bulls after a bloke like that taught you," said Pete warmly. "Look, Sam. How about coming down for a cup of tea and something to eat with us? It won't be very flash," he added apologetically, "But there'll be plenty of it."

There was no doubting the sincerity of Pete's offer and Sam was starving.

As they approached the house a small ragged fair-haired boy ran out to meet them and stopped uncertainly when he saw the stranger with his father. Then three more children came running round the side of the house. Two girls in this bunch, all with the same shy fair-headedness. Then came another one, a little toddler, partly hobbled by his fallen trousers.

"Struth, Pete," grinned Sam. "These all yours?"

"Yeah," blushed Pete. "We turned out six in the first five years. I did have it worked out how we fitted them all in but nobody believes us."

"Hell," laughed Sam. "At that rate you'll soon have the place stocked with more kids than cattle!"

PETE ATKINS'S PIGS

When Betty Atkins saw that she had a guest for lunch she almost panicked, much to Sam's private amusement. She flew round the kitchen kicking dirty clothes and pots and toys under the sofa, sweeping the dirty dishes off the table, throwing cardboard boxes and cut-up magazines and children with bare behinds into the hallway and putting on the kettle and food, almost simultaneously.

Sam liked her, in spite of her blushing confusion, which is really saying something for Sam.

A clean table-cloth was spread out and the best china and cutlery set in Sam's place. During the meal Sam helped himself to more tea and hot water from the kettle, cut himself and the children thick rough slices of bread and jam and made a mess on the clean table-cloth with a naturalness that put the whole family completely at ease.

After everyone had eaten as much as they could handle the children were sent out to play while Mrs Atkins cleared the table in front of the two men and did the dishes. Sam and Pete lit smokes and leaned back with a last cup of tea.

"What are you carrying most of here, Pete?" asked Sam.

"I've gone in for pigs the last couple of years," said Pete. "But I've had a lot of bad luck lately. I started off by fattening up a few wild pigs we caught in the bush up the back of here and got such a good price for them I decided to go in for it properly. But it looks as though I'll have to give it up."

"What's wrong with 'em, Pete? Prices no good?"

"No," said Pete. "The prices are good. It's the pigs themselves. I can't understand it. I bought some good breeding stock and spent over five hundred quid on sties to house them in. But they're dying on me for no apparent reason. It's even got the vet stonkered. They're getting plenty of good tucker, so it's not that. I'm beginning to think it must be something in the ground here."

"Doesn't sound likely," said Sam, "if you fattened pigs all right in the first place. Do you mind if I have a look at 'em?"

"Not at all," said Pete readily. "Have you had much to do with pigs?"

"Not a great deal," admitted Sam, "but it wouldn't do any harm to have a look. Used to be pretty interested in pigs once."

As soon as the two men appeared on the porch kids came running from all directions and ran ahead of them down to the piggery. Sam had a look through the pens and Pete introduced each pig more thoroughly than he had his family. He was obviously very fond of his pigs.

"Here's a young sow that just got crook for no reason," he said. "A kind of pneumonia, it is. But she's been kept warm and dry all the time. She'll probably die on me. . . . Here's a pen of baconers. Two of them went down with some kind of ear infection and now two more have got it. And the sties are cleaned out every two days regularly . . . And here is a breeding sow I paid good money for and she's lost every litter she's had. Premature. The old boar there is the only one that's doing any good, and he's out in the weather half the time."

Sam was looking through a mess of scraps in the bottom of the sow's trough.

"I see you've been feeding her on pumpkin," he observed.

"Yeah, that's right," said Pete. "It makes good pig-food. I buy up a truck-load of bad ones from the markets occasionally."

"That's probably why she's been slipping her litters," said Sam. "You never want to feed pumpkin to an in-pig sow. There's a kind of oil in the seeds that sometimes affects their breeding-gear. Some sows are more susceptible than others, but it pays to feed all your pumpkin to the baconers and play it safe."

Pete was stunned.

"Do you mean I've been causing it myself by feeding her pumpkin?" he asked in astonishment. "Why, I've had the vet up to look at that pig more times . . ."

"I'm only saying that that might be the cause," interrupted Sam. "And you can't really blame the vet for not thinking of it.

Today the vets are trained to use more drugs than common sense. It's not their fault. There seems to be a general distrust of anything old-fashioned, these days. If it hasn't got a scientific name as long as your arm it's no flamin' good. It might have its good points as a method of training but if you ask me they're breeding all the imagination out of the vets and doctors and everyone else in a profession. Those baconers of yours now. It's as plain as day what's wrong with them."

"What's wrong with them?" Pete was running out of exclamations.

"Who feeds them their milk?" asked Sam.

"Sometimes me, sometimes one of the kids. Why?"

"Well the way pigs crowd into the trough when they're being fed it's hard not to pour the milk all over them. And that's the one thing you've got to be careful to avoid. Pigs have very deep ears and when milk gets into them it stays in there and goes bad. That's where your infection comes from and that's what I mean when I say they're training all the imagination out of the modern vets. A vet in the old days would have picked that like a shot."

All Pete could say was "Well I'll go to hell."

"And this sty of yours," continued Sam. "It's a good building but a lousy pig-sty. The concrete floor's probably what's giving your pigs pneumonia, or whatever it is. A pig needs mud and space to move around in. Mud and pigs go together like bacon and eggs. How do you think wild pigs breed up so thick and healthy if they need concrete floors and a roof over their heads? I reckon if you extended these pens out past the concrete and gave your pigs plenty of mud and slush to root round in you'd cut your losses to practically nothing."

Pete was so excited he could hardly speak.

"We'll have to tell Betty," he almost shouted. "I don't know how to thank you, Sam. I don't mind telling you I've been nearly frantic . . . I'll tell Betty."

He practically ran into the house with a trail of children and Sam behind him.

"Everything's all right!" he shouted at his startled wife. "There's been milk in the pigs' ears and the big sow's been

221

eating pumpkins and there's oil in them and there's not enough mud and the vet's got no imagination!"

"Here," laughed Sam. "Take it easy. It's all guesswork, you know. It's going to take a fair while to find out whether you're on the right track."

"What's it all about?" asked Betty, completely bewildered.

"Sam knows all about pigs," said Pete a little more coherently . . . And bulls too!" he added. "Sam, if I could afford it I'd pay you . . . ar, hell!"

"Simmer down, Pete," said Sam. "As a matter of fact you could do me a real big favour."

"Anything you like," said Pete extravagantly. "Just name it."

"I've got a few days to fill in," explained Sam, "and if I get to where I'm going too soon I'll have to camp out because the accommodation won't be ready. If you could let me bunk down round the place and do a bit of work for my tucker I'd be real grateful. I don't want any pay."

"Hell, yes," said Pete. "I could even manage a few quid, I think."

"No," said Sam firmly. "If I earn any extra money before the end of this financial year I'll be up in another income-bracket and have more tax to pay than it'd be worth."

"We'll put Jimmy in with Nicky," said Pete, "and Sam can have the good mattress. We'll put it on the bed in the sun-porch and take Rose in our bed . . ."

He stopped then because both Sam and Betty had burst into laughter.

"What's so funny?" he asked.

"You are," said Sam patting him on the back. "At the rate you're going I'll have every bed in the place. You can give me a couple of blankets and I'll sleep right here on this sofa. And if I get any arguments out of you about it I won't tell you my secret formula for curing bacon on the hoof."

Pete talked pigs with Sam until nearly midnight that night. Betty came and dragged him off to bed eventually, but even that didn't stop him.

"Hey Sam!" he called through the house, just as Sam was going to sleep.

"Hullo," called back Sam.

"What was that stuff you rub on pigs for lice?"

"Linseed oil. Now go to sleep or you'll wake all the kids up."

THE REVEREND
MISTER CASH

Sam and Pete made some very drastic alterations to Pete's model piggery in the next two weeks. Then they ringed a paddock with pig-proof netting so the pigs could be let out for exercise. The improvement in the pigs was evident almost at once.

To Sam's vast amusement Pete kept inventing jobs he couldn't possibly do on his own to keep Sam's mind off leaving, but Sam was in no hurry for the time being.

The children thought he was wonderful. Probably because Sam made no effort to be over-friendly with them. Whenever he was around it was Uncle Sam this, and Uncle Sam that, with kids hanging all over him and his chair like blowflies round a dead horse. It got so that they wouldn't dream of going to bed without first saying a special goodnight to Uncle Sam, who told them an occasional story after tea.

"Why don't you two go to the pictures tomorrow night," said Sam rashly after tea one evening. "I'll throw the kids into bed for you. I'll bet you haven't been out on your own together for years."

"Oh we wouldn't dream of asking you to do that," blushed Betty.

"Yeah, I know," said Sam. "That's why I offered. You'll grow old too quick if you don't get a bit of a break away from the family now and then. As a matter of fact I've got a yarn to tell the kids I don't want you two to hear," he added. "You might learn too much for your age."

"Why don't you take the car and go yourself?" asked Pete. "We don't mind staying home with the kids, do we Betty?" he added carefully.

"Hell," said Sam. "I gave up going to the pictures years ago. I'd be bored to death. I never saw a film yet but what I couldn't have worked out a better line of bull for myself."

The car was barely out the front gate the next night before the kids were clamouring for a story.

"Tell us a story, Uncle Sam."

"Tell us a story about a horse. A white one!"

"No, tell us about goblins!"

"Tell us about God!"

"I want a story about God!"

"Here, here!" said Sam with a frown of annoyance that fooled none of them. "One at a time now.

"Tell us about God!"

"Well, I don't know much about God," said Sam. "Think of something else."

"Yes you do. Daddy says you know everything!"

"Tell us about God!"

"Well okay," said Sam, defeated. "I'll see what I can do. But no interruptions."

So with the Atkins's two-year-old on his knee pulling his tobacco-packet to bits and eating the bits, and their three-, four-, five-, six- and seven-year-olds crowding rapturously round, Sam told them about God.

"Quite a few years back, more years than anyone can count to actually, when all the land was still in scrub and bush and there were no fences or roads, there was only one bloke in charge of the whole outfit. In fact he was the only one in the whole world. That was God. There was a rumour that He made the world in the first place but there's been a bit of an argument going on about that.

"Anyway there was God, all on His own and He must have been pretty lonely on it because He imported a bloke and his missus. Adam and Eve — I never did hear what their surname was. He put them to live in a bit of an orchard He had. It must have been up round the tropics somewhere because they didn't need any clothes and if they'd been round here they'd have been frozen blue in no time.

"There was no work to do in this orchard. All Adam and Eve did was loaf round all day and eat fruit when they got hungry. That was most likely what caused the trouble because people with nothing to keep them busy always get bored and end up doing something they shouldn't.

"You see, there was a special tree in this orchard — an apple tree, I think it was — that God told them not to touch or they'd be

228

in for it. So what does Eve do? Being a woman she sneaks up one night and raids this special tree. Then she talks Adam into having a go at it too.

"People weren't so used to telling lies in them days and when God came to see how they were getting on He found out straight away that they'd been up to no good. Raided His special tree, in fact.

"There was a hell of a stink over it and Adam and Eve ended up getting themselves kicked off the place. They had to start from scratch on a place of their own and bring it into grass and fence it off to keep their stock in. That's how farming first started . . . I think.

"Then Adam and Eve had a couple of kids. Boys, Cain and Abel. I forget which was which but one of them was a proper mongrel. He finished up knocking his brother's block off with a hunk of rock and taking to his scrapers. And he never came back, as far as I can remember.

"Gradually there got to be more people but they were a pretty scraggy bunch and it wasn't long before God decided to do something to improve the breed. He bailed up a joker called Noah, not a bad sort of bloke, from all accounts, and put him on to building a dirty big boat. A monstrous thing it was. I've seen a photo of it. Somewhere. Took him years to finish it. Then he loaded samples of all the animals and birds in the world into it. Horses and lions and dogs and everything. I'll bet he had some sport keeping some of that stuff separated. Then he took on supplies of tucker and he and a few of his best behaved mates went on board and battened down the hatches.

"As soon as God saw that Noah was ready He started it raining — He can always make it rain if He wants to — and such a downpour you never did see. It rained for weeks.

"All the rivers and creeks came up and flooded the paddocks and washed out the bridges and still it went on raining. The water rose up over all the houses and trees and before long there wasn't an inch of land sticking up out of the water. All the no-hopers were drowned and all that was left was Noah and his mates and animals and things, floating round in his big boat.

"When God saw that everything was nicely flooded out He

229

turned off the rain and when all the water drained away . . ."

"Where did it drain away to, Uncle Sam?"

"Where did all the water go'?"

"Er — I think He pumped it all back up to heaven and stored it in big drums in case He wanted to use it again. In fact, whenever there's a big flood it means that someone's done something wrong and God has emptied out one of his big drums of water to warn us what happened last time.

"Anyway, all the people in the world today started from the ones that were on Noah's big boat and didn't get drowned in the flood. And judging by some of the ratbags I've run into in me time, I reckon old Noah must have had one or two stowaways on board."

"Is that all, Uncle Sam?"

"What happened after that?"

"Tell us some more about God!"

"There was a bit more to it than that," admitted Sam, "but that's just about all I can think of just now. There was a bloke called Jesus, who comes into it somewhere. He used to go round fixing up people who were crook and helping everyone out. They knocked him off round about Easter one year because they thought He was having them on. But apparently He was a fair-dinkum relative of God's, sent down to keep an eye on things for Him. They made a bit of a blue there.

"Now you kids had better hop into bed or I'll be in trouble with your mother. Hell, look at the time! Off you go now."

Half a dozen goodnights and a lot of tucking-in and drinks of water and trips to the toilet later the kids were all in bed and Sam sat back with a cup of tea in the kitchen.

"Must check up on what the hell did happen to all that water sometime," he muttered. "Don't want to be caught out on that one again."

Sam Cash, MP

"Are you coming down to vote in the big election on Wednesday, Sam?" asked Pete as they inspected a yardful of newly-marked calves.

"No, Pete," said Sam scraping mud off his boots on the bottom rail. "You and your wife go. I haven't cast a vote since they buried old Mickey Savage."

"Which crowd do you like this time?" asked Pete.

"None of 'em," said Sam shortly. "No matter who gets in, things are going to be just as big a muck-up as ever. One lot will slap a bit more on the Family Benefit and take it back off the tobacco and grog. If the other mob gets in they'll soft-pedal the Social Security and put a little back on our tobacco and beer. Politics in this country is just a matter of juggling a few million quid they haven't got . . . and talk, talk, talk. If you can bluff a man into thinking he'll be five quid better off if he puts you in a good bludger's job, he'll vote for you."

"I don't know, Sam. We couldn't do without a Government."

"Of course we couldn't," agreed Sam, "but the way they go about getting into power makes it impossible for them to do any good when they make it. They invent a phoney crisis to win an election and end up with a real crisis. They make impossible promises and get deeper in debt trying to keep them. They use up their overseas funds and blame the other mob for over-spending. If they laid off all their campaigns and advertising a couple of months before the voting, people would have a chance to work things out for themselves. The way things are most of the people vote for the ones who shout loudest, there's so much confusion."

"What do you think of Communism, Sam?"

"I don't know any more about it than the Russians," replied Sam. "But it'd be a real paradise for the bludgers, the way it sounds to me. No, the system we've got would work perfectly if it was handled right. You can bet your boots that the bloke who worked it out didn't mean the Government to take a hundred quid off our tax in one direction and slap it back on in another. That's not politics, it's juggling the books. Lawyers and accountants get put in jail for that sort of caper."

"But things have been improving all the time," protested Pete, who'd been very optimistically inclined since his pigs had come right.

"Not as much as you'd think," said Sam. "Everything must balance itself out. If you give a quid to someone you have to get it from someone else in the first place. If they'd had that one worked out properly we'd never have had a depression. They loaded money on one side of the scales and before they knew what was happening the whole works overbalanced and we were all in the cart."

"What about all the country the Lands and Survey Department is bringing into grass?" argued Pete. "Thousands of acres of it every year."

"Pete, old boy," said Sam, "for every acre the Government brings into grass I could show you two acres that are going back into scrub because there's not enough money to keep it going. Half the stuff they're breaking in was *in* grass a few years back anyway and had to be abandoned.

"A new set of spark-plugs is never going to fix worn-out piston rings, no matter how often they try it. There's a limit to what you can do with a forty million quid debt.

"No, Pete, when one of these political blokes faces up to things and comes and says: 'Look, Sam. We've got ourselves up to our necks in debt. The only way out of it is to lay off the spending for a couple of years and try to get everyone paid off' — *then* I'll back him to the hilt. But while they're trying to bluff me that they're doing a great job I'll dodge paying my income-tax as often as I can get away with it."

"You might be right at that," admitted Pete lugubriously. "But at least we haven't got any of them H-bombs to worry about."

"What the hell gives you that idea?" cried Sam. "We've got as much to worry about as any country in the world! More than some of them. We're the perfect target! Just the right size, nicely far enough away so no one else would get hurt, not important enough for either of the big outfits to start a war over. If the Russians wanted to demonstrate what they could do with a bomb as a warning to other nations, they couldn't do better than drop one fair in the middle of Lake Taupo."

"It can't be all that bad," said Pete unhappily. "They wouldn't do that to us — would they?"

"No one can be sure what they'll do," said Sam. "My guess is as good as U Thant's. You can't tell what a man's going to do when he doesn't know himself."

"I don't think I'll bother voting this time after all," said Pete. "It doesn't look as though it's going to be worth it."

"Of course it's worth it," said Sam slapping him cheerfully on the back. "You take your missus down there on Wednesday and cast the two deciding votes for Wally Nash. With all your kids you can use the child allowance he's promising us."

"But if the country's in such a mess . . ." said Pete dubiously.

"Pete old boy," laughed Sam, "this is the best little country in the whole world, and don't let anyone tell you any different. It's the freest, happiest, workingest, healthiest, pig-breeding-est place you could ever bring your kids up in!"

"But I thought you said the Government was no good?" exclaimed Pete.

"They might be no good at running a country," said Sam. "But when it comes to providing us with something to go crook about they couldn't be beat. And people with plenty of good healthy complaints are taking an interest in the country. They're happy people too. The only time people stop going crook about the Government is just before a revolution.

"Now let's turn these calves out and go up for lunch. I think Betty's got a quarter of mutton in the oven and I'm starving!"

Sam swung open the yard gate and Pete and he went laughing up to the house, with the kids running from all directions to meet them.

SADDLEBLANKET

Pete had knocked some skin off his knuckles stacking posts and he and Sam were walking back to the house for a cup of tea and a look at the pigs on the strength of it.

". . . Stank like an ensilage-pit and a face on 'im like a withered old mushroom," Sam was saying. "Saddleblanket, they called him, and a good name for the old sod it was too. He used to wander all over the place with a dirty big scythe, though I never saw him cut a blade of grass with it. Just used to carry it everywhere so he'd look as though he had something to do. And for getting himself knocked around I never saw the likes of him. He's the only bloke I ever knew who could get himself trapped in a chair while he was having his dinner."

"A chair?" exclaimed Pete.

"Yeah, an ordinary kitchen chair. Saddleblanket was having a feed in his hut one night and got both his feet hooked up in the rails of his chair. Still had his boots on and he couldn't reach round and undo them. Really locked there he was. It was lunchtime next day before someone heard him yelling and went over and let him go. Then the silly coot got his leg caught up in the top wires of a fence behind the church one night and fell over the other side. He hung there till they found him next morning. It's a wonder he didn't kick the bucket that time because it rained half the night. But he was a tough rag, Saddleblanket.

"Then there was the time he got caught in the window. A bloke going past in a car pulled up at the store and told them he'd seen a man hanging in a window on the side of a house a mile or so back. It could only be Saddleblanket so off we went to see what he'd done to himself this time. And there he was. He'd been standing on the sill of one of those big old double windows that slide up and down, trying to get them unstuck, he reckoned, but it wasn't his house and the owner was away in Dunedin. Anyway the top half of the window had slid down and jammed

Saddleblanket's fingers against the bottom half. Then the bottom half dropped on to his feet and he was stuck good and proper. He'd been hanging there for sixteen hours and was in a pretty bad way. One of the neighbours said he'd heard him yelling but thought he was trying to sing.

"It wasn't long before old Saddleblanket came right, but that state of affairs didn't last long. He was crossing a bloke's farm one day and noticed that a strong wind that was blowing at the time had pulled a haystack-cover loose and was whipping it to shreds. Being a good-hearted sort of a bloke, Saddleblanket decided to grab the loose rope and tie it down again. He was just reaching for the flying rope when it whipped itself round his wrist and before he knew it he'd been lifted fair off the ground and flung into a big old boxthorn hedge that hadn't seen the slasher for twenty years or more. He was in hospital for a long time over that little lot. I saw the hole in the hedge and it was hard to believe a little bloke like Saddleblanket could have torn such a terrific gap. Two of the ambulance blokes had to have thorns removed from their hands after just helping Saddleblanket up some steps.

"As soon as he came out of hospital again he got stuck right into knocking himself about, same as ever. He had more sticking-plaster than hide on him half the time.

"He fell into a big irrigation-ditch one night — full of eels it was — and couldn't climb back up the bank. He sloshed his way down it, waist deep in mud, for two and a half miles till he came to the road bridge and waited all night, ten yards away from an inspection ladder. The kids found him on their way to school next morning. He slept in some pretty odd bunks in his time, did old Saddleblanket.

"It got that way that you never cut down a tree, or let a bull out, or backed a truck up, or burnt off a patch of scrub without looking around to see if Saddleblanket was in the way first. Then he took on a job with another bloke demolishing an old mill and everybody reckoned that, with his kind of luck, Saddleblanket might just as well have put a bullet through his head.

"He survived two days on the job, but only just. They were lowering some big kauri beams they'd unbolted — about two foot square, they were — with a block and tackle. It worked okay at one end of the building but the floor was lower at the other end. They lowered a beam and found their rope wasn't long enough to reach the ground with it. So Saddleblanket grabs a timberjack and winds it up to take the weight off the beam while his mate hunted up a longer piece of rope. The jack, fully extended, was still a few inches short of the beam so Saddleblanket tells his mate to let her go and he'd catch the beam on the jack. When the beam hit the jack the handles flew round like aeroplane propellers. Knocked poor old Saddleblanket to bits. He had to be dug out from under the beam.

"One leg broken, one arm in two places and the other in one. One of his collar-bones was cracked, his jaw was fractured and every rib in his body was sprung. But he lived to see a good many more accidents.

"He had the doctors properly beat. He was upsetting all their calculations of how much punishment a human carcass can take. The District Nurse had put over nine hundred stitches in Saddleblanket's hide for minor axe and scythe and knife cuts that didn't require hospital treatment. She used to say that if you cut him into half-inch strips and put them in a sack and shook it up a bit, he'd come out without a mark on him.

"The only thing that seemed to weaken Saddleblanket was soap and water, but he managed to keep it at a safe distance most of the time. The last I heard of him was that he'd crawled under a bus for a snooze in the shade. The bus was hardly ever used but this day the regular bus broke down and they had to use it on the school-run. When they drove off Saddleblanket's coat got caught in one of the spring-shackles and he was dragged about a hundred and fifty yards before it tore loose."

"Did he get hurt?" asked Pete, who'd completely forgotten about his skinned knuckles.

"Too right he did," said Sam. "He was in a hell of a mess. But I believe they managed to patch him up okay. Unless he's been struck by lightning he must have more scars on him than the toe of a bushman's boot by now."

Back at the house Pete gleefully recounted to Betty Sam's yarn about Saddleblanket while she bandaged his hand. He always retold Sam's yarns, to everyone's vast amusement. He'd get carried away, once he got started, and exaggerate things out of all belief.

" . . . dragged him thirty miles along a concrete road until he fell off when they bounced over a railway crossing," he concluded.

"Really, Peter," giggled Betty. "I'm sure Sam never said anything of the sort. I don't know what the children are going to be like I'm sure. The things they've been coming out with lately! Rose says she's going to be a man like Uncle Sam so she can do everything and tell stories. Nicky's been gathering up dozens of old boards and putting them in a heap by the fowl run in case there's another flood . . . By the way, Sam, they want you to go and look at a dam they've built in the little creek by Muddy Gate."

"Yeah, sure," said Sam. "I wondered where they all were."

"I don't know what they'd do without their Uncle Sam," said Betty. "They . . ."

"You'll find out pretty soon," said Sam, not unkindly. "I'll be shoving off any day now. I promised a mate of mine up north that I'd be there to give him a hand with his mustering and he'll be depending on me to turn up. I've stayed here a lot longer than I should have really. It's been mighty kind of you to put up with me. But I'll have to get along."

Pete and Betty tried everything they could think of to persuade Sam to stay but he wouldn't budge from his decision.

"I'd be letting my mate down," he said. And that was that.

It was eventually arranged that as far as the kids were concerned Sam was just going on a long holiday and Pete offered to run him down to the railway station next day.

With surprisingly little fuss and embarrassment Sam shook hands with Pete on the platform of the station next afternoon and accepted a fiver of the twenty quid he offered him. As the north-bound express pulled away from the station Pete drove off home and Sam nicked across to the pub to fill in the hour and a half he had to wait for the next train going south.

242

SHABBY DOG

"Who's that bloke, Sam? asked Rube, poking his thumb towards a very thin and very long but not very tall man whom Sam had just spoken to briefly. Sam had run into Rube, a bloke he'd met briefly at Pete's place, as he came into the pub and was having a beer or two with him to pass the time.

"That's Dogs Bryce," answered Sam. "Never say anything about dogs in front of him. He's liable to do his block — whose turn to touch the kick?"

"Mine," said Rube, throwing a few coins on the bar. "Same again barman. Dogs eh? Why? Doesn't he like them?"

"There was a time," said Sam, shaking his head regretfully, "when Dogs Bryce was the best dog-handler in the country — probably in the world."

"That so?" said Rube, interestedly.

"Yes, Reuben Percival, that is so."

Rube glanced nervously around in case anyone had heard Sam and might think that was his real name.

"I can remember," continued Sam, "when Dogs was so good with dogs that it used to get him into more trouble than dancing three times with the same woman."

"How's that?" asked Rube incredulously.

"Well, he'd sell a dog to someone a couple of hundred miles away and two or three days later it'd be back at his place. They used to accuse him of pinching them back but it was just that they wouldn't stay away from him. You had to watch your own dogs when Dogs was around or they'd follow him home everytime. In fact it was a blasted nuisance whenever Dogs was leaving for home because all the dogs had to be caught and tied up till half an hour after he was gone.

"And while he was there all the dogs on the place would sit around looking at him as though he was a big lump of ripe horsemeat, though God knows there's not enough meat on his

245

skinny frame to feed one of them with a leg of mutton thrown in."

Sam absent-mindedly pushed Rube's change across the bar with his empty glass. "I've seen a litter of new-born pups crawl away from their mother and try to follow Dogs. He could break up two fighting bulldogs he'd never seen before with one shout. And if Dogs told one of his own dogs to sit and watch something he had to be careful to remember it or the dog would just sit there till it starved to death.

"He had to be barred from all sheep-dog trials in the country because nobody would compete against him after he cleaned up the field at Christchurch with a pig-dog he'd found on the road a couple of weeks before and trained up. Made everyone look real silly — whose shout is it?"

"Mine," said Rube quickly, putting more money on the bar.

"There was a rumour," went on Sam, "that Dogs once mustered eighteen hundred sheep off four and a half thousand acres of unfenced scrub and rock with an old fox-terrier and a one-eyed boxer.

"There were hundreds of theories why Dogs and dogs got on so well together but nobody was any more certain about it than Dogs himself. And if you ask me he didn't have the faintest idea. It was just one of those things."

"Well, how come he doesn't like them?" asked Rube.

"Oh he used to like them all right," said Sam. "Real keen on 'em. Wherever Dogs was there'd be dogs everywhere. It was one particular dog that ruined him. Made a proper goat out of him and he never got over it."

Sam emptied his glass, put it on the bar and reached into his pocket. "Must be my shout — blast it! I've left my roll in me other strides. Give us a quid, will you, Rube? I'll pay you back tomorrow. I don't like bludging on the drinks with me mates."

"Sure — here," said Rube handing him a note. "Is that enough?"

"Yeah, plenty," said Sam tucking the pound under his glass and nodding to the barman.

"What happened about this dog?" asked Rube curiously.

"Well," said Sam, "everyone around knew about Dogs and dogs, and dogs that nobody could do anything with were usually taken out to Dogs' place instead of being shot. Sometimes they'd buy the same dog back again after Dogs had made a dog out of it.

"One day a bloke rings up Dogs and tells him he's got a young bitch running around his place that they can't even catch, let alone do anything else with. It's a well-bred dog and they don't want to shoot it, so if Dogs can catch it he can have it for nothing.

"Down goes Dogs to this bloke's place and here's this bitch under the woolshed and nobody can get near her. She's timid all right. It took Dogs nearly twenty minutes to catch her and gain her confidence! She followed him home without a lead. A real likely-looking bitch she was, too.

"When Dogs got her home he went straight to work on her and inside a week she was one of the handiest dogs in the district. She'd head or hunt, back, pen up, muster on the blind and — I won't tell you some of the things that little bitch would do, Rube, because you'd just call me a liar. But by the time Dogs had had her a fortnight she was acknowledged to be as good as a sheepdog could possibly get, and she was still improving every time he worked her. Dogs even had his gates rigged up so she could open and close them. People came from miles away to watch her working. One bloke who was helping Dogs do a bit of dipping offered him five hundred quid for the bitch there and then, and the bidding was on. But Dogs wasn't selling.

"He was starting to get enormous offers for pups — even from overseas — and the value of the bitch was going up by about a hundred quid a day when the whole thing blew up on poor old Dogs."

Sam interrupted himself to say: "I think it's your shout, Reuben old boy."

"Yeah, yeah," said Rube putting more money on the bar. "Did the dog get killed or something?" he asked, glancing again at the man they were talking about, who was leaning on his own over a glass of stout on the other side of the bar.

"No," said Sam. "It didn't die and it's a crying shame it didn't. It would have saved a lot of strife by just quietly kicking the bucket. Old Dogs there would have been a different man altogether, instead of the wreck he is today."

Sam drank sadly from his glass.

"Well, what happened?" asked Rube impatiently.

"It started at the saleyards," explained Sam. "Dogs was a fairly modest sort of a bloke but he was naturally proud of having what everybody reckoned was the best dog in the world, so he naturally takes it to the sale with him. Besides, the dog was worth about three and a half thousand quid by this time and he couldn't risk getting it swiped. He was the centre of attraction down there with his famous dog.

"Then some sheep broke away from a mob that was being yarded — about twenty or thirty of them — so they let them get away a bit and then asked Dogs to put his bitch round them. Of course Dogs obliges. He put the dog out and then it happened — the best heading dog in the world casts out past the sheep and keeps going, straight for home! Dogs called and whistled but she didn't seem to hear him.

"There was a bit of laughing and scoffing round the yards and Dogs followed his dog home. When he got there he found that his troubles had only just started. The bitch had mustered all his in-lamb ewes and was trying to put them through the dip. It was a terrible mess. Seventy-odd sheep trampled and smothered.

"He sent the bitch round the front to try and break up the crush and she dashed off and brought in all the wether hoggets, over a thousand of them. And when Dogs shouted at her to come behind she nicked off and got the rams and piled everything up in a great mixed mess with Dogs yelling and cursing and not making any difference. He was still trying to drag sheep out of a heap in the corner where they were smothering themselves when the bitch turned up with forty head of cattle and an old draught horse from the back paddock.

"That little bitch turned on the best performance the world has ever seen or is ever likely to," announced Sam draining his glass and buying fresh drinks with Rube's change on the bar. "Dogs had no show of doing anything about it. Every head of stock on the place was crushing tighter and tighter into the yards, with the cattle treading his sheep into the mud faster than you could count.

"He ran up to the house and tried to ring his neighbours for help but everyone was away at the sale. By the time they got there three-quarters of Dogs's sheep were dead. They had to shoot the bitch before they could start sorting things out. It took days to clean up the dead sheep and cart them away.

"Dogs went to the dogs after that. He was never the same again. Just seemed to lose all his sting. In fact it's all he can do to get a dog to work for him these days. . . ."

Sam glanced suddenly at the clock on the wall. "Hell, look at the time! I've got to blow. Have to catch a train."

He drained Rube's beer by mistake, put the empty glass beside his own on the bar and shook Rube's hand.

"Been nice seeing you, Rube. And thanks for the loan."

And Sam was suddenly gone. Rube looked across at the brooding figure of Dogs Bryce, still leaning over the glass of stout.

"Poor devil."

A little later Rube was joined at the bar by a casual acquaintance. He ordered fresh beers and after a few moments of idle chatter he said: "You see that skinny bloke over there. The one drinking stout in the grey shirt?"

"Yeah."

"Well that's Dogs Bryce. He used to be the best dog trainer in the world but a bitch went crazy on him, smothered most of his flock. He . . ."

"Cut it out, Rube. That's Max Townsend. He's got a garage out near my place. I've been dealing with him for years. He's a bit of a live wire when he's had a few, liable to string you along a bit. But as far as I know he's never owned a dog in his life. He's been having you on!"

SIX OF ONE

It was a cold blustery night and to keep warm Sam got up and wandered around the deck every now and again. It was some time in the early morning and all the passengers had gone below to their cabins except Sam and the owner of the cigarette that glowed in the dark further along the deck.

Sam strolled along that way and sat down a few feet away from the cigarette and the dark blob of its smoker.

"Nice night for it, mate," he said conversationally.

"Yes," came the reply, and Sam stopped in the act of licking a freshly-rolled cigarette.

He was sitting next to a woman. A young one.

It was rarely that Sam was stuck for words, but it was also rarely that he sat himself next to young girls on dark boats.

"Er — what time do we berth in Lyttelton?" he asked awkwardly.

"Seven o'clock. A little later actually. We were late leaving Wellington and it's a rough crossing. . . . Did you think I was a man?"

"Ar — yes. As a matter of fact I did."

"An easily-made mistake," said the girl, or young woman, as Sam now realised she was.

"Have you got any idea what the time is?" asked Sam after a brief silence.

"Two thirty-five. Do you suffer from insomnia?"

"Never had a day's illness in me life," said Sam.

"Then why didn't you pay your fare and get a cabin?" she asked.

"Er — I have got a cabin," said Sam, "but I . . . What about yourself?"

This woman asked the damndest questions.

"Oh I sneak on without paying for the fun of it. Haven't you got any money?"

253

"Yes," said Sam. "I've got money, but I like to choose my own travelling companions. A man can't do much about his relations except keep away from them but he should be able to choose his company. The last time I made this crossing I was stuck in a cabin with a bloke who snored, a bloke who read comics and laughed all night, and a bloke who talked about his boss and his wife all night. I usually end up on the deck anyway."

"Yes I know what it's like. I make this crossing once a fortnight. How old are you?"

"Er — thirty-eight," said Sam. "What about you?"

"Twenty-seven. What do you do for a living?"

"Anything that needs doing," said Sam.

"Anything?" She was obviously sceptical.

"Well I couldn't remove a brain-tumour without a bit of practice," admitted Sam. "But I can handle most things."

"He was beginning to like this unusual woman with her audacious questions.

"Can you sail a small boat?"

"Yeah."

"A big boat?"

"Yeah."

"Can you drive a car?"

"Anything on wheels."

"Can you shoot?"

"Yeah."

"Fish?"

"Yeah."

"Build a house?"

"Served me time."

"Can you swim?"

"Yeah."

"Fight?"

"Yeah."

"Can you ride a horse?"

"Any horse."

"Can you iron clothes?"

"No. That's not a thing that needs doing."

"Well can you cook?"

254

"Yeah."

"Pastry?"

"Yeah."

"Can you sew?"

"Good enough to keep the wind out of me strides."

"Just as I thought," she said disgustedly, standing up. "A typical bloody man."

And she walked off leaving Sam sitting there wondering what the hell had struck him. He didn't know for a moment whether to be insulted or amused but his sense of humour soon had him grinning to himself in the dark.

"Cheeky mare," he muttered, rolling himself a fresh smoke.

A man in a dressing-gown came through a lighted doorway and out on to the deck.

"A bit warm for you down below, mate?" enquired Sam, who had completely recovered his good humour.

"Go to hell," snarled the man in the dressing-gown as he leaned over the rail to be sick.

Sam decided it was time for another turn round the deck.

Rounding a corner he saw a cigarette glowing by the rail and in case it was his woman friend he turned back and climbed a stairway to the deck above. He passed through a patch of light at the head of the stairs and hesitated as a familiar voice from the darkness ahead said: "It's colder on the other side of the boat."

"Yeah, I tried it," said Sam.

"Is there anything you haven't tried?"

"One or two things," admitted Sam jokingly. "But I'll get around to them sooner or later."

"Well how about trying to vanish," she said acidly.

He went back down the stairs trying to think of something he could have said and consoled himself with the thought that you can't insult anyone as crazy as she obviously was. He met the man in the dressing-gown in the passageway.

"Have you got any more of those smart remarks?" snarled the white-faced man pushing his way roughly past.

Sam shrugged away a faint feeling of persecution and went right up to the other end of the boat to look for somewhere quiet for a bit of sleep. The first corner he investigated had a broken bottle of wine in it and from the second a young man sprang out waving his arms threateningly.

"Get out of it, you blasted peeping-tom, or I'll knock your block off," he hissed savagely.

Sam's position on the boat didn't allow for him to be mixed up in a disturbance of any kind so he walked away and went right out on to the stern, where rows of cars were lashed to the deck. He was having a look at the latest Ford when "Hoi! What are you doing there?" called a voice from behind a torch that was suddenly shone on him.

"Nothing," said Sam.

"Well go and do it somewhere else. You're not supposed to be up here."

This was getting too tough altogether. Sam stalked angrily back along the deck and sat on a seat with his arms folded. Stowaway or not, the next one to insult him was going to be damn sorry for it!

But nothing happened and nobody came near him. Feeling a little foolish he uncrossed his arms and legs and rolled himself a smoke.

It was beginning to break daylight when he finally dozed off and ten minutes later a great milling mob of Girl Guides gathered on the deck near him to get their disembarking orders or something. Their giggling and chattering were ear-splitting. He moved away and leaned sleepily on the rail till the ship berthed an hour later, moving his position now and again as the gathering crowds drove him further towards the forbidden area where the cars were.

Then he almost missed the boat train into Christchurch when a lady in the most ridiculous hat Sam had ever seen insisted to one of the officers that he'd walked off the boat with her light-blue suitcase.

Sam was too weary to put up much of an argument and the case was found sitting on the platform just in time for him to stumble on to the train.

In Christchurch he couldn't find anywhere to buy breakfast so he sat on a bench and waited for something to open. And when he did get a feed it tasted like yesterday's leftovers. When the pubs opened he had two beers that tasted like yesterday's slops and then went and bought himself a ticket on the railcar to the West Coast.

"Your railcar for Greymouth leaves from here at two-thirty tomorrow morning," said the adam's apple who sold him the ticket. "Platform two."

Sam couldn't find anywhere to sleep during the day and by the time it got dark enough to lie down on a bench he was afraid to go to sleep in case he didn't wake up in time. As soon as the railcar arrived he got in and fell into a seat. At last he could get some sleep.

But Sam didn't reckon on the rowdy crowd of young skiers who were travelling on the same railcar to Arthur's Pass. They shouted and horseplayed up and down the carriage all the way and Sam had to abandon any hope of getting to sleep until they got off. Then another group of skiers, just as noisy, got on the return to Greymouth. So that was that.

When he stumbled blearily onto the platform at the end of the journey there was just enough daylight for him to see that it was drizzling with rain, had been for quite a while, judging by the amount of water that lay everywhere, and it wasn't going to stop just because Sam Cash had arrived.

He recovered two and a half hours of his lost sleep and a scrap of his optimism by the fire in the waiting-room and wandered along to a pub when they opened. A few beers restored him sufficiently to survive a long ride on the back of a truckload of deer-, cattle- and sheep-skins and by that night he was many miles away, sleeping peacefully at last in the shelter of an abandoned stone-crusher.

SOMEWHERE QUIET FOR THE OFF-SEASON

"You wouldn't care to stay and work on wages, Sam? asked Wally hopefully. "I've got plenty of work for you."

"No thanks, Wally," said Sam quickly. "I've finished my contract; now I'm off to somewhere quiet for the off-season." "What off-season?" asked Wally surprised.

"*My* off-season," explained Sam. "I have them quite often. It just means that I'm off work till I go broke again. Then I take out another contract. I might look you up on my way back, if I'm stuck for a quid," he added generously.

"Where are you heading for now?" asked Wally.

"There's a hut a bloke and I built on the Hakaroa Track in the Depression. It's somewhere on the other side of the range from here. I should make it in a couple of days' walk."

"What's the big attraction over there?" asked Wally.

"The big attraction over there, Wally old boy," said Sam, "is the fact that there's nothing to attract anyone else. The Hakaroa Track hasn't been used for twenty years and no one ever goes near the hut. I'll borrow a horse from the other end and pack in a few supplies. Then I can just loaf around and maybe shoot myself a few deerskins if I feel energetic. . . . There's only one thing that beats working for yourself."

"What's that?"

"Loafing for yourself. Now how about paying me for the job so I won't have to pester you in the morning."

"Okay Sam," said Wally resignedly. "I'll get you a cheque — but don't forget, there'll be a job here for you whenever you want one."

"Thanks Wally, I'll remember that," said Sam, shaking Wally's extended hand and wondering what the hell all the emotion was in aid of.

Sam left Wally Simpson's homestead early in the morning and

swung across the paddocks with a bag of gear on his back and a sawn-off .303 rifle slung over one shoulder. He settled into the long easy stride of a man who has a long way to go and half an hour later climbed the new boundary fence he'd put up for Wally and struck off at an angle towards a leading ridge that ran from the flats clear to the top of the range.

He climbed the three thousand feet in easy-looking stages that would have left many younger men gasping a thousand feet below him by the time he reached the top. After a smoke and a look at the view he crossed a late patch of thawing snow and began zig-zagging his way carefully down through the steep bouldery bush on the far side of the range. Some time in the afternoon he slid down a shingle slide into the headwaters of a little creek, which he traced on down the mountainside to where the Hakaroa Track crossed it on a couple of rotten logs. There he boiled his billy and rested contentedly against a rock smoking a well-earned cigarette.

A little later when the sun was climbing the far wall of the valley he spread his sleeping bag on a bed of fresh ferns and went off with his rifle to shoot a deer for meat. He didn't even see one, but that didn't matter to Sam. He'd pick one up in the morning, or some time.

A few thick slices of bread and condensed milk with plenty of strong tea made him a fair enough meal (a man's been eating too much lately, anyway), after which he lay on his sleeping bag in the firelight thinking "this is the life" thoughts.

Away again at daylight and shot a rubbery old stag for breakfast. Brains and liver with onions and toast. Then he shouldered his load and followed the unused track, winding down the valley side towards the coast. Over or under logs that had fallen across the track. Above or below slips that had scooped sections of it out of the hillsides. He carried steadily on down to where the track crossed the main river — an open ford, strictly for fine weather — and carried on along the other side for an hour or so and then crossed back again. He shot and ate a big brown trout for lunch.

The condition of the track became worse and progress was so slow by the middle of the afternoon that Sam knew he wasn't going to make the hut that night. So he just shot the next deer he saw and camped there. The hut was only half a day's walk distant. There wasn't a bootprint, axe-mark or fireplace or any sign of anyone having been there for years. Things were looking pretty right. It was just as he knew it would be, peaceful. Another week of Wally Simpson's wife and sister-in-law would have driven him crazy.

He strolled rather than walked next day and it was still cool in the bottom of the valley when he saw the clearing where his hut was, below and ahead of him. It was almost like returning home as he looked across the newly-remembered bushland. Things were a bit overgrown but otherwise exactly the same. He carried on towards the hut a little faster.

Sam stopped as suddenly as though a naked woman had just splashed across the creek and disappeared round the corner towards the hut. This was a bit boggy on it. The only hut for thirty miles and there's a woman there. A naked one! The best thing to do was make a noise and let her know he was coming, in case she hadn't seen him. He picked up his rifle and prepared to whistle as he walked towards the hut. Give her a few minutes to get a pair of strides on.

Then he heard a woman and then a man laugh not far ahead. He took a few uncertain paces and round the bend came three women and a man, strolling towards the far bank of the creek. All stark, motherless naked!

Sam pulled up with the suddenness of a man who's just run into a bunch of naked people on the forty-mile track to Hakaroa.

What the hell!

"Hello there," called the man, casually waving one hand. They continued picking their way tenderly over the stones towards where Sam stood wondering whether to dash into the bush or back along the track. It was too late. The women all made noises of greeting and they stopped a few feet from him smiling like clamshells.

"Come far?" asked the man.

"Er — ah — Wallaceville," replied Sam, looking at nothing in particular above their heads. "Heading for Hakaroa," he added.

"You'll find the track easy going from here on," said the man. You could tell he was used to organising things. "Call in at the hut and have a drink of tea. There's always plenty in the pot. One of the ladies . . ."

"Had a brew half an hour ago," lied Sam, far too quickly.

"Well," said the man, beginning to jig up and down a little, "we'd best be moving along. It's still a little cool for this time of year. Have a good trip now!"

And he led the three women briskly off along the track.

Sam moved across the creek and along towards the hut. Two men were throwing something back and forth in the clearing and three women sat on the porch reading. The very sight of them caused Sam to shiver. They waved and Sam waved back as he hurried past trying to look nonchalant.

The only way to handle this lot was to keep going!

He was just safely out of sight of the hut when he rounded a corner and stopped as suddenly as though he'd run slap into a naked woman painting a picture of a flowering rata beside the track. This one was cheating, she had a hat on.

By this time Sam was recovering from the shocks a little more rapidly and was able to answer her preoccupied "Afternoon" with a hoarse "G'day" as he strode past. And when he passed two naked men and a naked woman picking ferns and leaves a few bends further on he was no more nervous than a woman going for her first driver's licence.

He covered quite a distance by dark that night but saw no more of them. He sat by his little fire by the track working out what he would have said and done if they hadn't caught him by surprise. Blasted women! They were bad enough at any time, but running around in the bush with no clothes on! And keeping a man out of his hut that he helped build himself!

Must be one of them nudist mobs. But no one was ever going to believe a bloke.

HOKONUI HANK

"Pour us another couple, Sam, said the publican despondently, pushing the two glasses towards him. "We might as well get a beer or two out of the joint before she goes up."

Sam reached over the bar for the beer-hose and expertly filled his own and the publican's glasses.

"I reckon you might just be making a blue, Tom," he said. "There's been so many of these old pubs getting tragically burnt to the ground since the Licensing Commission weeded them out that the insurance companies aren't taking the old yarn about the drunk miner smoking in bed as much of an excuse any more. That truckload of furniture and the rest of your family moving over to Christchurch isn't going to stand much investigating either. Everyone from here to Springfield will have noticed it, and you'll be in real trouble if they rope you in for trying to defraud an insurance company."

"Things couldn't be any worse than they are," said the publican gloomily. "It's either that or bankruptcy."

Sam refilled his glass.

"Let's see what can be done about increasing your trade," he said.

"Not a hope in hell," said Tom ruefully. "I've been in hotels for thirty years and I know a dead pub when I see one."

"Don't be so sure," said Sam. "Let's work out what's wrong with the place and what can be done about putting it right."

"I've already told you," said Tom wearily. "You can't sell beer to people who aren't here. When the mill closed down everyone moved away; so did all my regular customers."

"That leaves the passing traffic," said Sam thoughtfully.

"That's out," said Tom decisively. "There haven't been more than two cars a day in here on the average since they altered the main road and cut off this loop. I spent fifty quid on those signs out there and another hundred and seventy on getting the road done up. People just won't go out of their way for a drink when they can get it on the main road a few miles further on. No, the only thing to do is to put a match to the bloody place."

"Hmm," said Sam thoughtfully.

"Anyway, tourists passing here," continued Tom, "are always in a hurry to get down to the glaciers or back home. They never stop for more than one or two drinks in any case."

"Hmm," said Sam again.

"Nope, this pub was built for the mill and road gangs. Now they're gone there's nothing left but for the pub to go too."

"It's a pity you couldn't have hung on for another few years," said Sam. "Once they get the road from Paringa to Haast finished there'll be more traffic on this road than you could keep track of."

"Yeah, I know," said Tom dejectedly, "but I couldn't hang on for another week, let alone years."

"Give it another week, Tom," said Sam, as though suddenly coming to a decision. "You've got nothing to lose and I think we might just be able to boost things a little. The trouble with this pub is that it's too much the same as any other West Coast pub. I've never run across a tourist yet who didn't think they were different from all other tourists. We'll make a few alterations and give them a pub that's different from all other pubs — and keep them here once we get them into the place."

Tom was only too happy to seize at any chance to save his pub but he was still pessimistic.

"I'd like to, Sam," he said, "but I'm afraid it's no go. I couldn't afford another penny on alterations. I'm up to the eyeballs in debt as it is."

"The alterations I've got in mind won't cost you a cracker," said Sam. "Just give it a week of your time and if business hasn't picked up you can throw a match into her."

"Okay, Sam. You're on."

Sam became very businesslike. He filled the glasses again.

"Right," he said. "Has this district got any local history? Like murders or hold-ups and things. That's one thing tourists really go for."

"None whatever," said Tom shaking his head regretfully. "It's eight years since we even had a road accident."

"Good," said Sam. "We can slap a bit of scandal on to the place without any facts contradicting us. Have you got a rifle round the place?"

"Only an old army job," said Tom. "It wouldn't do to hang on the wall. Everyone round here has got one."

"Just what we want," said Sam. "Bring her out, and about twenty rounds of ammunition."

Tom fetched the weapon and a handful of bullets. Sam stuffed several into the magazine and led the way outside. After looking all round the building Sam stood outside the bar, about twenty yards away, and jacked a bullet into the breech. Then he raised the rifle and fired a shot straight through the bar-room door. Glass tinkled inside as the bullet shattered bottles on the shelf behind the bar.

"What did you do that for?" asked Tom in a shocked indignant whisper.

"That," said Sam slamming another shot through the wall, "is where an old bushman called Hokonui Hank bailed up in the early days after he'd killed his mate" — another shot through the doorjamb — "with an axe after they'd been on the Hokonui whisky for a few days."

Another shot through the wall. It ricocheted off the fireplace and sang round the bar-room.

"These bullet-holes are where the police were trying to smoke him out. I think another couple through the door and one or two in the other wall ought to do the trick — and perhaps one through the sign over the door."

"But look what you're doing to me pub!" protested Tom.

"It's nothing to what you were going to do to it," said Sam, casually firing a couple of bullets through the lavatory for good luck. "If those tourists don't come here in droves to actually see the bullet-holes where a gun battle took place in the early days I'll go out of the business-rejuvenating business."

Tom grinned and then chuckled as the logic of Sam's theory dawned on him.

"By the powers!" he said. "I think you might be on to something. But what if someone checks up on it?"

Sam took careful aim and raked a long bullet furrow through

269

the wooden step into the bar.

"Nobody is going to check up on the evidence of their own eyes," he said. "In fact everyone who sees these bullet-holes and hears the story of Hokonui Hank is going to become an authority on it when they get back home. They'll add a bit of spice here and there till we won't recognise the true yarn ourselves. All you'll have to do is play the incident down a bit as though it was an unpleasant disgrace to the district and even the locals will start to believe it. Within six months you're going to have at least half a dozen eye-witnesses and no end of old blokes who used to work with Hokonui Hank. He'll probably become a bit of a hero and there'll be fights when some stranger says something bad about him. You'll probably be able to look up his birth certificate and police record within a few years. We'll just start off the tale and leave the date, his personal appearance and other details to the local old-timers."

Inside the bar they found such a scene of wreckage that it was hard to believe a gun battle hadn't been fought there. Several bottles were broken on the shelves. A long deep gouge ran right across the bar. The door and window-frames were beautifully splintered and the walls from then on were obviously going to be described as "riddled".

Sam poured two beers and while Tom cleaned up the broken glass and spilt liquor he "slapped a bit of age on the bullet-holes".

"A neat little bit of work," said Sam proudly, stepping back to admire the last time-worn, mud-dabbed furrow in the mantelpiece. "Tomorrow we'll see about baiting the trap."

Sam was awakened next morning by the sound of a rifle shot. He went to the window of Tom's best bedroom — nothing was too good for him as far as Tom was concerned — and was just in time to see his host fire another shot into an old army hat on the gravel driveway.

"Hey," called Sam. "What the hell are you up to?"

Tom looked up. "I'm just fixing Hokonui Hank up with a hat," he grinned.

"Well don't overdo it," warned Sam. "It's going to be sticky enough convincing people who've been here before that those bullet-holes have been in the bar-room all the time, without having hats and bloodstains and things to explain away.

"After breakfast we'll take a bit of gear down to the main road and rig those signs a bit better."

They loaded paint and brushes, an axe, a shovel, hammer and nails and themselves into Tom's station-wagon and drove the quarter-mile down the hill to the turn-off.

"Look at that," said Sam, climbing out and surveying Tom's big new sign. "WELCOME TO WHITE-PINE HOTEL (200 yards) THOMAS BINE, LICENSED VICTUALLER," he read out.

"Yep," said Tom, "the one at the other end of the loop is exactly the same. Cost me fifty quid to get 'em put up. Hasn't made any difference to me trade though," he added ruefully.

"And no bloody wonder," said Sam. "A tourist wouldn't take any more notice of that thing than if it was an extra leaf on the tree it's nailed on to. Where they come from they see flash signs everywhere they look every hour of the day. We'll fix up something that'll really catch their eye."

So they painted over Tom's flash fifty-quid signs and Sam drew in big, rough, dripping letters: TOM BINE'S BOOZER (½ Mile) DRIVE CAREFULLY.

Tom's lack of enthusiasm was distinctly noticeable.

"I don't think that's much of an improvement," he said dubiously.

"I should hope not," said Sam. "It's not supposed to be an improvement. It's what you might call a strategic retrograde step. There's so much improvement going on in pubs nowadays that they're improving all the atmosphere out of them. And what do you think people go to pubs for?"

"To drink, of course," said Tom.

"That's where you're wrong," said Sam. "If people only wanted to drink they could do it a lot cheaper and easier at home. No, it's the atmosphere and the company that makes the pub such a popular place. I'll guarantee there's more mileage clocked up in going back and forth to the pubs every year than there is to church or the beaches or visiting relatives or any of the things people do for the hell of it. That sign now, it suggests atmosphere, and it's your job now to see that the customers aren't disappointed."

"But what's the idea of the drive carefully bit? I've had the road done up. It's in perfect condition."

"It won't be when we've finished with it," said Sam. "Let the fern grow over the sides and the wash-outs wash out, and the surface get boggy. Drop a tree across it and clear it away just enough for a car to get past, and what have you got? You've got atmosphere, that's what. When a tourist gets to the pub he's going to feel like he's discovered a forgotten hunk of history tucked away in a remote corner of Westland. He's also going to want to celebrate. It won't be long before everyone is saying: Have you been in to Tom Bine's boozer? You haven't? Well you'll simply have to see it, etcetera, etcetera."

On the way back to the pub Sam undid a bit of work on the road with the axe and shovel to give the erosion a start.

After lunch they were putting some local colour into the general appearance of the hotel, Sam with an axe and Tom with a pot of roof paint, when the first customer drove up in a muddy Land Rover. They went into the bar to see his reaction to their handiwork. A man in shorts and big boots came in tucking in his shirt.

"How are y', Tom?" he said familiarly. "What have you done to your sign down there?"

Then he saw Sam and nodded.

Sam nodded back.

"Meet Sam Cash, Doug. Doug Pettigrew, our Public Works man," introduced Tom pouring three glasses of beer.

Sam and Doug shook hands.

"Please to meet y', Sam."

"Same here," said Sam.

"What happened to your sign?" repeated Doug. "And what the hell happened in here?" he added looking round at all the bullet-holes.

"Er — that's where Hokonui Hank got shot at by the police," said Tom awkwardly.

"Cut it out," said Doug incredulously. "Who are you trying to kid? Those holes weren't there the day before yesterday. Hokonui Hank!" he snorted.

"Well actually it's to attract tourists," said Tom as though he'd been caught cheating at cards.

"The tourists!" cried Doug. "What tourists? There won't be any tourists on this road until next November. And then there'll only be a handful of them. What's got into you?"

"We just thought the place needed a bit of atmosphere," said Tom miserably, looking towards Sam for support, which he didn't get.

"Well you've sure got it," said Doug, "but what good it's going to do you I don't know. . . . No, I won't have another beer thanks. It's too draughty in here. And I have to get up to Greymouth before the shops close."

And he went out and drove off, leaving Tom completely crestfallen and Sam completely unconcerned.

"Doesn't look as though it's going to work out like we planned after all," said Tom unhappily.

"No," said Sam helping himself to another beer. "It's going to work a lot better than we planned. Once it gets around that you've shot the pub full of holes to attract the tourists, people are going to come for miles to see for themselves. And that means we've succeeded in getting more customers, whichever way it works. We'll just sit back and wait for them."

Tom was unconvinced, and Sam was right. First it was a Forestry gang. Then a group of deerstalkers, who stayed for four days when Sam organised a shooting match with a dozen of Tom's beer for a prize, which he won himself. Then farmers and bushmen from forty, fifty, and sixty miles away dropped in to have a look and joke about Tom's Hokonui Hank story, which changed drastically every time he told it.

Then on a long weekend all the traffic had to be diverted to pass Tom Bine's Boozer because an enormous beech had mysteriously fallen across the main road. Someone mentioned hearing an explosion in the middle of the night but it was put down to the effects of Tom's hospitality. Then the Public Works DETOUR signs vanished and after that they were often seen set up diverting traffic past Tom's pub when business was a little slack.

One quiet afternoon Sam and Tom wrote hundreds of fictitious names, addresses, and dates all over the wall around the fireplace. At first the regulars — there were quite a number of them by this time — scoffed and joked about Tom being a bull-artist and a leg-puller but, as Sam predicted, they soon began to write their own names on the walls.

"Now you're getting atmosphere," said Sam, pouring himself a fresh beer.

Tom Bine's Boozer became a milestone on the coast road. Everyone discovered that it was halfway between their place and somewhere else and seldom went past without calling in for a beer and to see what the hard-case Tom Bine was up to now. People left messages there and Sam announced that that was the best indication they'd had yet.

Sam calmly kept himself in the background and his glass full unless he was needed, and seemed to Tom to regard the whole miraculous process as something of a joke.

The legend of Hokonui Hank was trotted out for the entertainment of any stranger who had the time and interest to listen to it, but by this time Tom's account had become so extravagant that nobody was ever likely to take it seriously. What had become almost legendary, however, was the yarn of how Tom Bine had tried to start one by shooting his pub full of bullet holes, which was better still.

"Y'know, Sam," said Tom at breakfast one morning six weeks after Sam had arrived there and asked for a beer and the weather forecast, "I'm thinking of sending for the wife and kids. We've turned over eleven hundred quid in the last month. I'm not out of the woods yet but if this keeps up it won't be long before I've got me head above water again. You'll get along fine with me wife. I've written her all about you."

Sam grunted nothing in particular and went out to have a look at some possum traps he'd set in the bush behind the pub.

Sam's last customer that night was an Acclimatisation Society ranger who was on his way up to Westport. Tom had gone to bed two hours before and left Sam to close up. So he did.

He stuffed a handful of notes out of the till into the pocket of Tom's sports coat and then put it on. Then he scribbled a note and left it on the bar under a bottle of whisky: "Been called away, Sam." Then he switched off all the lights, locked up, and dropped the keys in the window before closing it.

As they drove away, the ranger, who'd been waiting in the car for him, said "They tell me this Tom Bine is a bit of a hard case."

"He's a hard case all right," said Sam. "Some of the things he gets up to would have you in fits — but he's no bloody good at putting a yarn across," he added with more emotion than the remark seemed to call for.

HOME

Sam dug spuds for a week on the Canterbury Plains and then flew across Cook Strait in a Viscount because he didn't go for the type of people who travelled on the ferry these days.

In Wellington he drove a fork-lift on the wharf till he had his plane fare to Auckland and a few quid to spare. Then he boozed it up, borrowed a fiver off a taxi-driver he'd met and caught the bus to Napier.

He operated a drag-line for a Napier firm until he had enough money to pay his plane fare from Napier to San Francisco, and that got him as far as Gisborne. He cut lawns for the Gisborne Council for a few days, sold the mower to a publican who'd done a mate of Sam's for his cheque in the old days, stole it back, drew his pay and caught the bus to Opotiki. Sam distributed a good slice of his hard-earned cash among the publicans of Opotiki and decided to make a straight dash for it, to get home before he went broke again. So he set off to hitch-hike north and very soon got a lift to Whakatane. That night he was in Tauranga, the guest of a shopkeeper who'd picked him up at Matata and taken an immediate fancy to him. For the price of listening to an endless round of bad and badly-told jokes, Sam got a feed, a bed on the sofa and a lift to Paeroa the next day.

"It's only about forty miles from here out to the main highway," said the shopkeeper, shaking hands with Sam at the turn-off. "You'll have no trouble getting up to your place by tonight," he added. But he was wrong — it took Sam two months to get from there to his "home", a house his wife lived in that belonged to his father-in-law, who didn't think Sam was everything a son-in-law should be by a long shot.

Sam strolled along the suburban road from the bus stop, past the neat rows of houses with trimmed gardens and lawns and hedges, until he came to the right number. After looking round the garden for a few minutes he went inside. His wife was at the kitchen sink.

"Oh," she exclaimed when she saw him, "you did give me a start! Where on earth have you been?"

"Have I got a clean shirt?" asked Sam, lifting the lid of a steaming pot on the stove and sniffing the contents.

"Look at you!" she cried. "Filthy! I just hope none of the neighbours saw you like that. You just get straight into the bathroom and give yourself a thorough going-over. Then you've got some explaining to do. You can't come in here after five years asking for clean shirts. The cheek of you!"

Sam went into the bathroom, rinsed his hands under the tap, shook the water off them and patted them half dry on a clean towel. Then he went into the sitting-room and began to build a fire out of the heap of smouldering sticks in the grate.

"You've burnt me bit of wood I use for a poker," he said. "When will tea be ready?"

"Tea will be ready when it's cooked," she said sharply, coming to the sitting-room door. "You needn't think you can march in here and order tea whenever you like — I knew you'd be back as soon as a bit of extra money began arriving. I know you, Sam Cash!"

Sam had pulled up a chair and sat in it with his feet on the mantelpiece.

"How about swingin' the billy?" he asked, getting out his tobacco.

"I'll put the kettle on when I'm good and ready," she said, going into the kitchen and putting it on. "You can't come lording it round here just because I haven't seen you for five years. You're lucky I'm still here. Daddy offered to pay for a holiday in Australia for me. I nearly went, let me tell you."

"You've planted flowers in me lettuce-patch," said Sam.

"Of course I have!" she said indignantly. "Do you think I'm going to keep your lettuces going for five years while you loaf around the countryside, hardly ever working, not sending any regular money — where have you been, anyway?" she demanded.

"There and back," said Sam. "And I might have to go out again later, so see if you can hurry that tucker up a bit will you, I'm starving."